Father's Day

A.T. Nicholas

Father's Day

By

A.T. Nicholas

A.T. Nicholas

Special thanks to God and the Lord Jesus Christ who always had good advice.

A big thank you to my kids, Alex and Alaina for showing me what pure joy feels like, and Anita for many great years of support and love.

Special note: To my parents, thank you for always being there for me and for always being a great example throughout my life. Your words taught me well, but your actions and the way you lived your lives was the greatest teacher, and it made all the difference. I love you both very much.

To my brother Bill, no one could have a better brother, friend, and the occasional substitute father when Dad was hard at work. I want you to know I'm grateful for the sacrifices you made for me, and that I love you. Thank you.

Thanks to my family and friends that helped and encouraged me. Thank you, Tiffani Jill for simply being a part of my life. Special thanks to author Clint Cassa for all his help and feedback. Thanks to John Zuknick for introducing me to a wonderful editor, Stephanie Fallon.

I would like to also thank William D. Van Wie and District Creative Printing for all their help in the past and future projects.

A.T. Nicholas

1

Lachesis muta, also known as the Amazon Bushmaster, is one of the most dangerous snakes in the world.

The six-foot venomous serpent slid effortlessly across the undergrowth of the rainforest without a sound hunting for prey in the darkest hours of night. The Bushmaster's flickering tongue gathered airborne particles, its unblinking eyes absorbed infrared rays radiating from warm-blooded animals, its senses felt the slightest vibration, and its half-inch fangs were ready to sink into the skin of its next victim.

The cold and graceful reptile moved quietly past another dangerous predator hidden within the lush green foliage. Only inches from a Naval SEAL commando's face, the snake slithered by, never detecting the soldier lying in wait.

Lieutenant Gill had been waiting twenty-nine hours under camouflage netting in the deepest part of the Amazon rainforest, along with eleven of his friends. They had been watching a building, which was submerged beneath the tropical vegetation, its roof hidden by the natural growth of the rainforest's surroundings. The SEAL team would had never discovered it if it weren't for satellite imagery, hard work, long hours, and most importantly, a good old-fashioned traitor.

Inside the building resided a group of terrorists. The leader was a man named Abas Majlis, aka the Scorpion. Majlis was believed to be responsible for the death of six thousand United States citizens throughout the world, including the three terrorist attacks on American soil. He had murdered men, women, and children. He had killed government officials and military personnel. His range of victims had no boundary.

Lieutenant Gill and his men were watching the building seventy-five yards away, through infrared scopes on their weapons. A group of terrorists, three holding flashlights began to exit. The last man to step out was Abas Majlis the Scorpion.

Lieutenant Gill flicked the safety off his weapon.

All eleven of Gill's men knew the plan. Once the Scorpion was in view, Gill would take the first shot, which would start a simultaneous killing. But the Scorpion must be taken alive.

Seconds after the Scorpion stepped out into view, the three terrorists holding the flashlights had bullet holes in their heads. Nine more were down before the flashlights hit the ground. The Scorpion and two of his men escaped the fate of their companions by diving back into the building.

The twelve-man SEAL team moved in. One commando blew the door off the building. The narrow corridor was dark, but not to the SEAL team wearing night-goggles.

As he entered, Gill got the sensation of being in a sewer hunting rats. The corridor was barely wide enough for two commandos to stand side-by-side.

Gill led the team with two of his men flanking him a step behind. The last two to enter had the rear covered. The team reached a closed door. Gill passed the door followed by the two flankers, who watched the far end of the corridor. With hand signals, Gill instructed two men into the room.

One of the commandos kicked in the door and quickly stepped aside. He leaned against the wall, staying out of the line of fire. Slowly he moved into the dark room followed by another commando, and then a third. They searched the area through the multi-green-colored world of their night-goggles. There were nearly fifty different shaped boxes stacked throughout the space, which appeared to be used for storage.

A terrorist sprung up from behind a pile of boxes. His pale green image was perfectly clear to the commando. He screamed, "Death to America!"

"Bomb!" one of the commandos yelled as he fired into the man's chest.

The terrorist squeezed a device in his hand detonating a bomb seconds before he hit the floor.

The room instantly filled with a blinding explosion of heat and killed two commandos. The SEAL team positioned in the corridor felt the wave of heat roar out of the room and the six-inch-thick stone wall shake violently.

A burst of gunfire sounded from the far end of the corridor.

One of the commandos spun and fell to the floor after taking bullets to the arm and shoulder.

Three SEALs opened fire on the terrorist.

Bullets tore into the walls, spraying concrete in every direction. The terrorist disappeared into a doorway.

The three commandos ran along the corridor, quickly closing the gap between themselves and the terrorist's position.

One of the terrorists stepped out into the corridor and fired blindly, wounding one of the commandos. Gill fired four shots, and the terrorist dropped to the floor dead. He rushed down the corridor and leaped over the dead man. He leaned against the wall beside the doorway and yelled in Arabic, "Majlis, drop your weapon!" He heard the shuffle of footsteps in the room, but no response. Gill's voice softened. "My boss wants you alive, so why don't you do us both a favor, and come on out?" he continued in Arabic. The room remained silent. "Come on, Scorp, don't make me carry you out of this jungle in a body bag. You're about a hundred fifty pounds, right?"

"A hundred and sixty-five," Majlis answered.

"See what I mean?" Gill said. "That's way too heavy for someone my age. I'm not a young man anymore. I can't carry dead bodies like I used to."

There was movement in the darkness. It sounded like someone searching for an exit only to discover there wasn't one. The next minute was quiet and no verbal response.

"OK, here's the deal," Gill's voice turned hard. "We have three options. One, you blow yourself up like your buddy back there. Two, I put a bullet in your thick head and take you home in bubble wrap. Three, you walk out peaceful-like and we fly first class back to the good old US of A. Personally, I don't care which one it is, but I can guarantee one thing. It will be one of the three."

After a short moment of silence, a weapon slid out of the dark room across the floor.

"They said you were a smart man," Gill said. "I'm starting to believe them."

2

The dark room flickered with light from the television. The volume was too low to be heard clearly. Slumped on the couch was a man reeking of whiskey. In one hand he held a gun, and in the other, he carefully clutched a hand-drawn Father's Day card made by a five-year-old boy. The man painfully stared at the bright red and staggered written words, "I LOVE YOU DADDY." The pain was replaced by a whisper of a memory. In his mind, he could clearly see a proud little boy presenting the card and a man expressing his joy over-enthusiastically. Like a million times before, the whisper was drowned out by the screaming anger. It had become relentless and had forced him to the darkest place he had ever been. He raised the gun and stared at it as if it were the solution. The screams of anger and pain could be silenced in one swift moment. Now the gun was against his temple and his eyes were closed. But for some reason, he could clearly hear the voices on the television. He opened his eyes and focused on the words, "BREAKING NEWS" across the screen. The broadcaster announced that the notorious terrorist Abas Majlis, the Scorpion, had been captured. He slowly pulled the gun away from his head and it silently rested on the couch.

3

One Year Later: Washington, D.C.

Private Investigator Art Hanson stepped through the large oak church doors. His brown shoes squeaked slightly on the luminous white and cream marble-floored corridor. On the left side there were stained glass windows portraying Biblical events. When the sunlight filtered through them they exploded brilliantly in a vivid display of color. Lifelike statues of saints carved of ivory colored marble lined the right side. Art tipped his fedora at the saints. "Nice to see you boys again," he said. His brown suit was straight out of a forties Humphrey Bogart movie. He was average in height, but built solid. His bushy sideburns, thick mustache, and aged eyes made him appear older than his fifty-one years. He continued along the corridor and occasionally glanced up at the large stained glass windows. Like a hundred times before, he passed the life-size marble statues of saints lining the hall and warmly greeted them by name the way one would acknowledge a living person. He opened a door that led down to a sub-level floor where his good friend Professor Gregory Orfordis did most of his private work on ancient scriptures.

"Professor O, you down here?" Art asked in a voice that sounded like he smoked since birth.

The room was softly lit by candles, which made it difficult to see clearly. But the real challenge was the old rickety stairs he had to climb down.

"Over here," his seventy-year-old voice came from the darkness, "by the cabinets."

"What's going on?"

"I'm gathering a few documents for my trip."

"Let me guess," Art said smiling with his cigar tucked in the corner of his mouth.

Art was never without a cigar in his mouth, lit or not. He called it his blankie; Greg called it a pacifier.

"Israel," Art continued.

Greg's soft wrinkled face grinned. "Your private investigative skills never cease to amaze me."

"Well, Derrick left yesterday, I had a feeling you'd go after him. What makes you think he'll talk to you over there? He hasn't returned your calls in what, eight months."

"I must continue to try," Greg said earnestly.

The man they were talking about was Derrick Moore, the President of the United States and a close friend of Greg's. But nearly a year ago Derrick had become distant, and in Greg's opinion transformed from a caring man of God to a self-absorbed, power-addicted totalitarian.

"Regardless," Greg said, "I must find a way to speak to him."

"Is there anything I can do?"

"I don't believe there is."

"If you need me, let me know," Art offered. "I only have one job at the moment."

"What is it?"

"This lady called me a couple of days ago and said she hasn't seen her ex-husband in nine months. She seems worried he did something drastic, like offed himself."

4

Isaac Van Gins was his new name. The old one died with the man who a year ago held a gun to his temple and nearly pulled the trigger. The new man was a volunteer at the Baltimore Aquarium. He was one of the scuba divers that cleaned the shark tanks. The old man had a sickness so toxic that it ate at him until a shell of a man remained. And then, the new man was born and he was filled with anger and vengeance. The other man and his reason to live were left mangled beneath a mountain of smoldering rubble.

Van Gins stepped off the bus and walked the last mile to work, no different than he had done the past year. But today would not end like any other, today a shock wave would be sent around the world, and an old wound would begin to heal.

*   *   *

Dunkirk, MD

A.T. Nicholas

Terri Hutch, an attractive thirty-two year old daycare provider walked out of the center and crossed the parking lot to meet a man that was leaning against an old beat-up car. "Why are you here?" she asked calmly.

The man shoved his hands into his blue jeans. "Because I love you," he said staring at the ground. "I want to come back home."

"I can't go through this today," she said. "I have to get all these kids ready for a field trip to the Baltimore Aquarium."

He looked up at the cloudless blue sky. "Perfect day for a field trip."

"Just sign the divorce papers Jimmy," she pleaded.

He kicked a small stone and looked at her coldly. "No way in hell I'm signing those damn papers."

The other daycare providers and twenty young children were gathered at the windows watching the couple in the parking lot.

The last time Jimmy showed up the police had to be called. He wasn't happy with the separation and Terri kicking him out of the house. One day he had too much to drink and tried to convince her to let him come back. When she refused he became verbally abusive and was bordering on becoming physical.

Terri's coworkers started to move the children away from the windows and one of them picked up the phone.

"It's not fair." He didn't try to hide his irate tone. "You get to stay in the house and keep the Mustang. I get to drive my mom's junker and live in her basement. You throw me out and that's it, right?"

Terri's eyes narrowed. "I didn't sleep with someone else," she said with her lips tight.

A.T. Nicholas

The shame surfaced in Jimmy's baby blue eyes. He stared at the ground again attempting to hide it. "One mistake and it's over," he mumbled.

"The one mistake I can't forgive," she said sadly.

He looked up and said, "I can't stop loving you."

"Were you loving me when you were with your girlfriend?" It wasn't her intent, but her words came out razor sharp.

The shame turned to defensiveness. "I'm not with her anymore," he said loudly. "I love you."

A deep sadness fell over Terri's face. She looked him in the eye. "But I don't love you." She started to back away. "Just leave Jimmy, please."

"I'm not signing the papers," he said pointing his finger at her.

She walked back to the center. She heard the car door slam and seconds later the tires burn off down the parking lot. She never looked back.

* * *

Annapolis, MD

I sank into my overstuffed lawn chair and lit a fat Padron cigar. I tilted my head upward and allowed the warm June sun to hit my forty-five-year-old face. The sweet sound of Smoky and the Miracles was on the radio. Days like this made me think about retirement, but I loved my work too much to stop. Five years ago, I was put in charge of the Hostage Rescue Team, a tactical unit within the FBI. I have had five hostage situations since becoming Commander and each time I successfully negotiated a positive outcome. That meant the hostages lived and the bad guys didn't. There was one situation that the FBI screwed up, but I didn't want to think about that now. So the thought of retirement quickly passed. Plus, I was too young. I stretched out my six-foot frame and ran my hand through my graying hair. At least I still had it all.

From my elevated deck, I watched a neighbor float past in a sailboat on the South River. Larry the lawyer glanced up at me from his thirty-something-foot weekend toy. He didn't wave. I guess he was still mad at me. Larry invited me to one of his parties with a bunch of his lawyer buddies, and naturally I decided to tell a lawyer joke. "What happens when a lawyer takes Viagra?" I asked them. "He gets taller". I thought it was funny, and so did the wives. Anyway, no more party invitations for Adam Turner, and obviously no neighborly wave.

A slight breeze shifted directions and the mouth-watering aroma of a perfectly aged sirloin steak filled my nostrils. "The sweet joys of a day off," I said to myself. "A fine cigar, a cold beer, and a juicy steak." Then my mouth cracked into a grin. "Damn, it's good to be the king."

I took a drag from my cigar and watched the smoke from the grill stream into the blue sky. It was time to eat. I put the tender steak on a plate and let it stand for a moment, allowing the juice to sink into the meat. Now I needed a side dish. I returned from the kitchen with another beer. I looked at the lone steak on the plate and the beer. "Perfect." The knife cut through the steak effortlessly. My mouth was watering with anticipation. I forked a healthy size piece of meat and slid it into my mouth. I chewed with my eyes closed, forgetting the other four senses existed. "The sweet joys of a day off," I mumbled.

My cell phone rang in mid-chew. I stared at it as if it were another predator attempting to move in on my kill. The incoming number on the screen embodied a very large rain cloud, threatening my perfect day. It was work, and if work was calling me, something really bad had happened.

"What?" I answered.

"We have a hostage situation," the voice on the other end said.

And just like that, the clouds formed into a wicked storm and the perfect day was over.

5

Baltimore, MD

"What the hell is going on?" Art Hanson asked himself, stopped at a red light.

Ten police cars sped by nearly sideswiping his car.

Art turned down another street and three more emergency vehicles screamed past. He poked the buttons on his radio reaching for a news station. He heard a helicopter fly overhead. Finally a voice on the radio announced that the Baltimore Aquarium had been locked down. "Terrorists? Maybe another psycho shooting up the place?" he thought. He also remembered the Aquarium was only five minutes away.

Art parked his car and walked down the sidewalk to a small row of brownstones. "Tiny place, big money," he thought. He rang the doorbell.

"Yes," a woman's voice crackled through the intercom.

Art pushed the button. "I'm Art Hanson, a private investigator. Can I ask you some questions?"

"About what?" she asked guardedly.

"Are you Pamela Robertson, the sister of Hank Robertson?"

"Yes," she answered without hesitation.

"Can I come up?"

"What's this about?" Her voice became fractious.

"I guess not," Art thought. "Mr. Robertson's ex-wife April hasn't seen him for nine months and she's starting to worry," he said attempting to reflect the ex-wife's concern.

"I haven't seen him for nearly a year," she quickly fired back.

I haven't seen him could mean three things; she hadn't seen him, or she had and was lying, or she hasn't seen him but had other means of contact. "No phone calls or emails?"

"No," she answered decisively.

"OK, thank you for your time," Art tried to say as pleasant as he could. "I'm going to leave my card in the mailbox just in case he contacts you. Have a nice day."

The intercom was silent.

"Alrighty then," he mumbled to himself.

Art sat in his car and wrote a few notes down on a pad of paper. He wasn't sure what to think of the sister, but he did know one thing, she was lying. He asked too many questions in his life not to be able to know when someone was lying, even if it was a little white lie.

6

Baltimore, MD

I pulled my dark blue SUV onto the sidewalk a hundred yards from the Baltimore Aquarium and shook my head in disbelief. The chaotic scene was overwhelming. Thousands of people were as far as the eye could see in every direction. I had never witnessed anything like it. This scene dwarfed the bank robberies and domestic situations I had worked on in the past. Statistics showed the larger the crowd and the more media attention there was, the faster the hostage taker became temperamental and suicidal with the negotiations. This could become really bad, really fast.

I stepped out of my vehicle wearing black flame-retardant overalls, bullet-proof vest, multi-pocket tactical vest, assault boots, and thigh holster armed with a .45 ACP loaded with 230-grain Hydra-Shok hollow-point bullets. Just an hour ago, I was wearing a tank top, shorts, and flip-flops.

A twenty-eight-year-old man raced across the Inner Harbor courtyard toward me. The closer he got, the more apparent it was that he was an operator from my assault unit. William Jones, the youngest man on the team, but had been with my unit the longest. He wore a patch on his sleeve that separated the HRT from the other similar dressed special operations groups on the scene. He, and like myself, wore an insignia of a flying eagle clasping a steel-linked chain in its talons with the Latin inscription that read, *Servare Vitas*. The translation was, "To Save Lives."

"Sorry," William said.

"What are you sorry for?" I asked as I surveyed the grounds.

"Its steak and cigar day isn't it?" William asked.

"Steak sandwich and cigar day, to-go," I said walking toward a Baltimore City police officer. "Where are we?" I asked William.

William quickly ran through the status at the scene. "SWAT secured the inner perimeter. The command post is setting up over there," he said pointing to a large truck.

I got the attention of the police officer. I instinctively glanced at the officer's name tag. "Officer Parker, I need a favor."

"Yes, Sir," the officer said, immediately recognizing the patch on my sleeve.

"Pass the word along with your guys that I need to see anyone who has information on the gunman."

"Yes, Sir." The officer reached for his radio.

"Thanks," I said and turned to William. "I need the floor plan."

"Got it."

"Any injuries?"

"None to report."

"Any contact with the HT?" I asked concerning the Hostage Taker.

"Nothing."

My phone rang. "Adam Turner," I answered as I continued to walk.

It was SOC, Strategic Operations Command. They were on the scene and searching for the best location to set up command post on the outer perimeter.

I turned to William. "It's SOC, they need a location."

"Tell them to set up shop at the Hard Rock Café across from the Aquarium."

I passed on the information and stepped into a large black and white truck. It was a high-tech mobile command post that would be used as the Tactical Operations Command. The truck was equipped with every communication capability available to the human race, and every level of surveillance equipment tax-dollars could buy. The rest of my team would gather there to formulate a tactical plan.

The truck door opened and one of my men poked his head in and said with a grin, "Hey, Commander, Officer Parker has your witnesses."

I stepped outside and was greeted by a daunting sight. I was looking at over a hundred people. "Officer Parker," I said.

"Yes, Sir."

"I need another favor."

"Yes, Sir," Parker said, ready to go.

"I need you and your guys to interview these people. I need identities and descriptions of the HT and the hostages, I need a head count, weapons count and type, location in the building, and anything else you can get."

"We're on it," Parker said turning to start.

"Move them to the outer perimeter," I added before returning to the truck.

I started to study a map of the city trying to get familiar with the surroundings. I needed high buildings with good locations for my snipers, and a potential offensive strategy for entering the building.

A few moments later there was a knock on the door. One of the operators answered it and found a security guard holding a large brown envelope in his hands.

"The man in the aquarium told me to give this to whoever was in charge," the security guard said nervously.

"Commander," the operator yelled, "we have a situation."

I walked over to the door and saw the security guard and the envelope. He was sweating and his eyes were pleading for me to take the envelope away from him. I said as calmly as I could, "I need you to back up about twenty-feet and set the envelope on the ground."

The security guard backed up slowly and carefully set the envelope down. Then he continued to back away.

"William," I called, never taking my eyes off the envelope. "Take this gentleman away from here and find out what else the HT had to say."

"Joe."

"Yes, Sir," the operator said stepping next to me.

"Get the TEU on the phone," I said. "Tell them we might have a CB situation. Call the bomb sniffers, too."

Everyone understood the situation had escalated. They knew I was thinking chemical or biological agents, or a bomb and that meant it was time to call in the Technical Escort Unit.

7

Annapolis, MD

Art Hanson sat in a popular downtown pub in historical Annapolis drinking a beer when he saw former FBI analyst Kelsy Anderson cross Main Street. He hadn't seen her for weeks and was looking forward to getting together again. They had become good friends over the past year while working on a dangerous case. He also viewed her as the child he never had. He watched her approach and noticed her hair wasn't strawberry blonde anymore, but a light auburn. She still had the shapely five-foot-seven frame that got plenty of attention from the boys. Her bright blue eyes and smooth Irish skin had remained youthful throughout her thirty-two years.

"Hey, Art," Kelsy said with a hug.

"What's up with the hair?"

She ran her fingers through it. "Do you like it?"

Art grinned. "You'd look good bald."

She laughed. "I don't know about that."

"Have you heard from Mary and Allen?"

"They're still in Greece," she answered.

"Are you kidding," he said shaking his head. "It's been nearly a year."

"They said they were taking a long honeymoon."

"They're not coming back are they?" he said jokingly.

"Maybe to visit." Kelsy sat across from Art and pulled a small notepad out. "This guy Hank Henry Michael Robertson, you wanted me to check out for you, appears to have packed up and headed for the Caymans."

"Really," Art said.

"About a year ago," she read from the pad. "He transferred an undisclosed amount of money to a Grand Cayman bank account. Around the same time he withdrew thirty thousand dollars in cash within a span of two weeks. He also renewed his passport and bought a one-way ticket to the Caymans. The plane ticket was the last thing he bought on his credit card before he canceled it. I don't know if he got on the plane or not because I couldn't find any passenger records. He paid off all his bills and discontinued all services to his house. He left the house to his sister to sell."

Art thought how nice it was to have a friend who had FBI connections and also worked for a secret agency called White Cell that could tell you how many times someone hit the snooze button on the alarm clock before they got up. "His ex-wife said he quit his job about the same time all of this was going on," he mentioned.

"It sounds like your case is solved," Kelsy said. "The guy decided to retire and live the good life."

"He was a helicopter pilot for shock trauma," he said. "Maybe he had enough."

"I'm assuming he didn't fill the ex-wife in on any of his plans."

"She doesn't have a clue."

"Did she say why she was worried about him in the first place?" Kelsy asked putting her pad away.

"She said he was depressed," he answered. "I figured he didn't take the divorce very well."

"Sounds like he found a cure for his depression."

"I'll pass your information on to the ex-wife and see where she wants to go from there," he said, and then a big smile appeared beneath his bushy mustache. "Maybe she'll want me to go to the Caymans and check up on him."

Kelsy smiled back at him. "I think I should tag along. You might need back-up."

"You're right," Art said becoming serious. "I could use you for those hard to reach places on my back."

"You should never underestimate the seriousness of sunburn."

8

Baltimore, MD

I watched the Army helicopter from Aberdeen Proving Ground, Maryland land at the Pier 4 parking lot from my command post. I also could see all the media cameras focusing on the new situation developing, and whatever was about to happen was going to play out on live TV. The ten-man Technical Escort Unit filed out of the side wearing bright yellow coveralls. Some of the specialists carried radiation and chemical-detection equipment. Others held mass spectrometers and portable isotopic neutron spectroscopic devices. A very intimidating sight, I thought. My stomach turned from the bad thoughts sneaking into my mind. The team was there to detect, contain, neutralize, and dispose of the threat. If that wasn't possible, then it became damage control. It was that last part, the damage control that was bothering me.

They split into five separate pairs and encircled the envelope with a thirty-foot perimeter. Two of the specialists aimed a fluorescence device at the envelope and waited for a reading. Within moments, one of the men shook his head "no", meaning there were no chemical or biological agents in the package. One of the specialists removed a cylinder tank from his back. If needed, he would had sprayed the package and enclosed the dangerous agents in dense foam.

Another specialist maneuvered a remote controlled vehicle fitted with an X-ray system. The two-foot by one-foot vehicle had the appearance of a toy truck, but this toy cost as much as a live size truck. The operator positioned it near the envelope and a screen plate deployed over the package. The first reading was negative. The specialist read the screen on his control once more and then gave the "no bomb" signal.

The commander and one of his men moved in toward the envelope. The two remained cautious. The TEU had a cardinal rule: never trust the equipment completely. They both wore explosive armor beneath their chemical and biological coveralls, and I was hoping the gear wouldn't be tested today. The two men were briefed on the helicopter that the envelope was handled without incident, but they approached the package as if it were armed with an explosive.

I watched the commander and his man move in on the package for a hands-on and visual confirmation.

One of the specialists remained ready with a spray gun loaded with liquid nitrogen that would freeze any trigger mechanism and electronics.

The commander of TEU carefully lifted the envelope and examined it before he finally unsealed one of the ends and inspected the contents. A moment later the two men pulled off their breathing apparatuses and gave the rest of the team the thumbs up.

The TEU leader waved me over. He smiled and declared the package disarmed. "There's a disk and a sheet of paper in there." He handed the envelope to me. "I hope I didn't contaminate any evidence."

"Don't worry about it," I said grinning. "Thanks."

"Piece of cake," the TEU specialist said with a wink. "We're going to set up a few CA monitors around the perimeter just in case. Now if you'd excuse me, I need a drink, or two."

I carried the envelope with my gloved hands to the command post to examine it for fingerprints, hair fibers, skin tissues, and body fluids. I would also watch, listen to, and read the contents. And hoped some of these pestering questioning in my head get answered.

9

Art sat at the stoplight on State Circle and searched the radio for the latest news on the hostage situation.

"Right now, all we know is," the voice said over the car radio, "a group of children and a teacher are being held hostage in the Baltimore Aquarium."

"Unbelievable," Art mumbled to himself. He parked his car and walked into the Marriott Hotel in downtown Annapolis. He made his way through the restaurant to the outdoor bar and sat next to the ex-wife of the missing man. "Thanks for meeting me," he said.

"No problem at all, Mr. Hanson," April said.

"Please, call me, Art."

"What would you like to drink?" the bartender asked.

"Same as the lady."

"Did you find Hank?" she asked optimistically.

"Well," he started to say. "I did and I didn't."

"I don't understand."

"That's why I thought it would be better if we talked face to face." Art pulled his notepad from his jacket. "You see, I believe he's in the Caymans somewhere."

Her eyes widened slightly with disbelief. "Why do you think that?"

"He transferred some money to an account in the Caymans. He also withdrew a large amount of cash and renewed his passport and bought a one-way ticket to Grand Cayman."

"Wow," she said taking a sip from her drink.

Art took a big swig from his drink and nearly choked.

The bartender brought him a vodka and tonic.

"Sorry," April said. "I should have warned you. I figured you thought I was drinking water."

"Yeah," Art said catching his breath.

"I guess that's it," she said. "He went to the Caymans."

"It looks like it."

"I wish he told me," she said, turning her head away from Art.

Art handed her a napkin and she wiped the tears from her eyes. "I would like to do one thing before I close the book on this," he said. "Can I go by his house and take a look?"

"Sure," she answered. "Why?"

"Maybe I can find something that will tell me where exactly he is," he explained. "And maybe I can talk to him and let him know you'd like to talk to him."

"You don't have to do that Mr. Hanson," she said, wiping her eyes.

"Art," he insisted again. "I don't mind, if you don't."

"I would like to know he's all right."

"Great," he said throwing a twenty on the bar.

April pulled her keys out from her purse and slid a single key off. "This is the house key." She wrote down the address of the house on a napkin.

"I'll call when I have something."

"Thank you, Art," she said warmly.

Art walked to his car and wondered what happened to their marriage. He wanted to ask her, but didn't feel right.

10

Baltimore, MD

I sat in front of the video equipment waiting for the disk from the envelope to load. I had already read the list of demands that came with the disk. The HT wanted a limousine, a motorcycle, an armored truck, a boat, a car, and a helicopter. He was specific about the type of each vehicle and where to park each one. I had sent a copy of the demands to the Strategic Operations Command post and strongly suggested they start shopping.

"Sir," an operator said, walking into the truck with a sheet of paper. "Here's the list of employees of the aquarium."

I took one look at the list and shot a look of incredulity at the operator.

"Six hundred volunteers," the operator informed.

"The teacher and the kids?" I asked.

"We still don't have a name for the teacher," the operator reported. "We're working on the list of kids and their parents."

"We need the teacher's information and all the parents of the kids," I said. "We need to start eliminating as many suspects as possible, as soon as possible."

The operator disappeared out of the truck.

I turned to the screen and found a figure of a man from the waist up wearing a black ski mask, sunglasses, and black coveralls staring back at me. I pushed the play button.

"No one will die if you meet my demands," the HT said in a distorted voice.

I hit pause. "We're going to need to clean this up."

"It sounds like some cheap voice altering device," the operator said. "It won't take long to get his real voice."

I continued the video.

"There's a list of demands in the envelope," the HT said. "But if something happened to it and it has become unreadable, this is what I want."

The HT described the type of vehicles he wanted in detail, exactly identical to the demands on paper.

"If you need to contact me," the HT said. "You can send someone to the east-side loading dock with a cell phone or any other means of communication you prefer."

"I need a secured two-way."

The HT's gloved hands came into view and pulled the top of his coveralls apart, exposing a mechanical device taped to his bare white chest.

I hit pause and leaned forward in my chair. "What the hell is that?" I said as I printed a still photo of the image. I hit play.

"Semtex Plastique," the HT said. "Enough on me and around the building to take out five-square blocks. If I stop breathing, boom."

I stopped the video. "Brief the others," I said. "Tell the snipers we have a loaded target."

"I also sent a copy of my demands to the media," the HT announced.

"Great," I mumbled.

"The copy the media has is similar to the copy you are watching. But the media's copy says I want a million dollars for the hostages. I don't want a million dollars, I want something else in return for the lives of the children."

Everyone in the room locked onto the screen. I could feel something bad was coming.

"I want Abas Majlis, the Scorpion," the HT demanded. "You have till eight o' clock tonight. Don't make me kill children."

The figure of the man was gone and the disk went blank.

"Lord help us," someone in the room said.

"What a nightmare," another operator said under his breath.

I checked my watch and leaned back in my chair. "Roughly six hours."

"We can't give him Majlis," an operator said.

"He thought of everything," I said. "He tells the media he wants a million dollars so if we meet his demands, we can save face. No one would know we released a terrorist leader for the hostages. But if we don't meet his demands, it looks like we wouldn't give up a measly million bucks for a bunch of kids."

It wasn't up to me if Majlis was released to him or not. He was the FBI's property now. But I had this strange feeling settling in my gut. The only way I could describe it was relief.

11

Bowie, MD

Art and Kelsy pulled into a community of small houses fifteen miles outside of Washington, D.C. The homes sat on quarter-acre lots and were well kept with the exception of the house they approached. The landscaping and lawn were neglected. There were children playing in the other yards and neighbors exchanging warm conversation. In contrast, the house they pulled up to appeared lifeless.

"My guess," Art said. "That's the house."

Kelsy checked the address on the notepad. "You're so good."

Art knocked on the door and rang the doorbell. "Just in case," he said smiling at Kelsy. "I don't want to surprise anyone."

After a few moments, he slid the key into the lock and opened the door. A musty odor welcomed them with a rude embrace.

"Wow," he said turning his head attempting to get fresh air.

"Nice," she said, putting her hand over her nose and mouth.

Art tried the light switch. Nothing. They would have to use flashlights and open the curtains for light, and try to ignore the smell.

Art aimed his flashlight at a pile of mail scattered across the floor under the mail slot. "Looks like some people didn't get the message."

"I'm going take a look around," Kelsy said.

"I'll check the mail, maybe there's something useful."

Kelsy carefully searched around the dimly lit house. The rooms were still sparingly furnished. There were clothes thrown throughout one of the rooms, which she determined to be the master bedroom. The other room appeared to a child's. There was a small bed and sports theme décor on the walls. "Did the ex-wife say anything about having a kid?" she yelled down the hall.

"No, she didn't," Art yelled back.

She moved into the kitchen and found the source of the bad odor. She discovered more than thirty old half eaten frozen dinners on the counters and in the sink. Empty bottles of hard liquor were also scattered about. She searched the drawers and found nothing unusual. Kelsy examined a notepad she found on the counter near the disconnected phone. There was nothing written on any of the sheets, but she saw an impression left behind from the last thing written. After she found a pencil, she smudged the lead with her finger, and exposed a readable vision of what was written on the previous page. The name Jack and a phone number stared up at her from the pad. She dialed a friend at the FBI.

"Hey, Larry," she said. "I need the location of this number." She read off the digits.

"Hello to you too," Larry said jokingly.

"How are you doing, Larry," she asked politely.

"I'm doing fine, thank you. How are you?"

"Good, thank you."

"Key West," Larry answered and then gave her the exact location.

"Thank you," she said. "You're a sweetheart. I'll buy you lunch."

"Yeah, yeah," Larry laughed. "You owe me a year of lunches."

Kelsy called the Key West number.

"Hello," a man's voice answered.

"Hi, Jack," she said in a sweet tone.

"Yes, Ma," he returned the sweetness.

"Is Hank there?"

"Hank?" he asked confused.

"Hank Robertson."

"Oooooo," he said suddenly remembering. "No, he's not down here. Who's this?"

"Kate, his girlfriend. I thought you guys were going fishing."

"Not me," he said. "I don't fish. I don't understand why he would give you my number. I'm supposed to buy a car from him. Maybe he meant to give you my buddy's number."

"He hasn't sold you the car yet?" she asked, trying to gain more information from Jack's statement.

"No. He said sometime this month."

"You think he gave me the wrong number on purpose?" she said jokingly.

Jack laughed.

"Who's number I'm supposed to have?"

"Paul," he answered. "I set up a fishing trip for Hank on Paul's charter."

"Can I have Paul's number, please?" she asked, "unless there's some kind of guy-code not allowing you to give the girlfriend the number."

"Just don't tell him you got it from me," he joked. "Is there something wrong with Hank's phone?"

"I think his cell has poor reception down there," she said, and then she laughed and added. "Or he's avoiding my calls."

Jack laughed and then gave her Paul's number.

Art was listening to Kelsy work the phone while he dug through the mail. He found among the junk mail a notice from a storage company in Kill Devil Hills, North Carolina. It informed Hank Robertson that his storage unit and a number of other units were burglarized. The storage business was also requesting his presence to verify any missing property and to contact his insurance company if needed.

"He has a storage unit in Kill Devil Hills, North Carolina," Art told Kelsy.

"He's supposed to sell a car to someone named Jack in the Keys and he also chartered a boat with someone named Paul."

"Now what?" he asked.

"Let's take another look around here," she answered. "I'll call my friend Larry and have him get some info on Jack and Paul from the Keys."

12

Baltimore, MD

I stood up from the screen and placed my weapon on the desk and grabbed two hand-held two-way transmitters. I had decided I was the one to deliver them to the HT. There were plenty of volunteers, but I rejected them. I didn't know what it was, but there was something bothering me about the HT. There was a nagging voice deep in my mind trying to tell me something, but I just couldn't make it out.

"No weapon?" William asked.

I glanced at my gun on the desk. "Don't need a gun," I said and pointed to my head. "I got this."

William gave me dubious stare. "Try not to get a bullet through it."

"Sir," a young operator said. "I have the voice of the HT, but it sounds like he disguised it with another sound modifier. When we get it cleaned up, a voice analysis possibly could match it up."

"What did the bomb guys say?" I asked.

"They said they were ninety-nine percent sure it's the real deal, but they couldn't confirm the set-up. They also said, assume the HT was telling the truth."

I closed my eyes and thought of the damage the bomb could do. I didn't like the image I saw.

"I also found something else. There's a slight delay between his voice and his mouth on the video. It's obvious he did it on purpose."

I smiled and shook my head. "If we tell the public we didn't meet his demands because he wanted Majlis, and show the video of his demands for evidence, it looks like we tampered with it."

"I could fix it," the operator suggested.

I stared at him. "No," I said quietly under my breath. "I bet the media's copy is in sync and no mention of Majlis."

"We're back to the million dollars."

I stepped out of the command truck into the hot and sunny day. I looked around the harbor at the thousands of people gathered around the outer perimeter and stared at the media tent with discouragement, knowing I would need to address the situation to the public and the media at some point. My head hurt just at the thought of it.

"Commander," another operator said, handing me a sheet of paper. "That's the list of parents of the kids."

I allowed my eyes to scan the long list of names. "Unbelievable," I mumbled.

"Yes, Sir," the operator agreed. "We're working on the biological parents first, then to the step-parents. So far, we can account for six biological and one single parent."

"And the teacher?"

"Nothing." The operator reached for his beckoning radio. "Go ahead," he answered.

"We have more parents showing up," the voice on the radio announced.

"I'm on my way," he said. "I'll brief you after I talk to them." The operator started to walk away, but turned for a moment. "Commander."

I looked up from the list of names.

"Don't be a hero."

I smiled. "That's my line."

"Yeah, and don't forget it."

I made my way to the aquarium and approached the loading dock entrance with the hand-held transmitters. I glanced to my right and off in the distance, about two-hundred yards away was one of my men positioned on the roof of a building. To my left was another sniper watching every move through the scope of his rifle.

The large metal door began to open upward. The black boots of a man appeared first, and then slowly his entire body was standing in the open.

I was ten feet away from the HT. He was a big man, maybe six foot four and two-hundred thirty pounds.

"Who are you?" the HT asked with no emotion in his tone.

"I'm Adam Turner, the Commander of HRT," I answered, trying not to sound hostile.

The HT stared out at me from the black ski mask over his face. I saw him glance down at my empty gun holster, and then at my hands. "Is that how we're going to talk to each other?"

I looked down at the transmitters. "If you want."

The HT walked over and stood in front of me. I could feel the cross hairs over my shoulders.

In situations like this, there was always a shade of fear in everyone involved. Fear was what kept you sharp; fear was what kept you alive. I saw no fear in this man's eyes. I also had no fear of this man and I didn't know why. I took a mental note of the color of his eyes. I decided they were grayish-blue, and there was no indication of bluffing in them. There was something else in his eyes, but I couldn't find the word to describe it. They were telling me something. I also couldn't figure out what the voice in my head was trying to tell me.

The HT held out his hand.

I handed him one of the transmitters. "Channel one."

The HT looked around at the buildings, and then asked with a quiet voice, "Do you think they're itching to put a bullet in my head?"

I looked around at the snipers on the rooftops. "They prefer everyone walk out alive."

"If I get Majlis, everyone lives," the HT said in a much colder tone.

"I'm working on it."

"And the vehicles?"

"That's on schedule."

"I need the people delivering the vehicles to dress alike, and then I want them to meet in the Aquarium Café and wait," the HT demanded. "They also need to bring me extra clothes. The clothes need to be exactly identical to what they are wearing."

"Sure," I said. "Anything else?"

"Don't make me kill these kids," the HT said turning to leave.

The large metal door started to close.

"Do you have a name?" I asked.

"You can call me," the HT started to answer, "Mr. Parrot."

The door closed with a loud crash.

I stood for a moment staring at nothing and thought about what the HT said. "Mr. Parrot," I said to myself out loud. The voice in my head got a little louder.

13

Kelsy stood on the stoop in front of Hank Robertson's house holding the notice from the storage business in North Carolina. She also had Jack and Paul from the Keys rolling around in her head. She felt unsatisfied with Art's missing person case. When she felt this way there was only one thing to do, get satisfied.

"Feel like taking a drive?" she asked.

"Sure," Art answered with a grin. "Where to?"

"Kill Devil Hills, North Carolina."

"Needing some closure?"

"I'm curious," she said almost defensively.

"Rrrrright, curious."

They started walking to the car. Kelsy turned and stared at the house. Something was eating at her and she had no idea what it was. Whatever it was, it made her unsettled and sad. And she didn't like it.

"Are you all right?" Art asked.

She didn't realize it, but she had been thinking of her father. "I was thinking about my dad," she said still looking at the house.

Art watched her. He knew something was bothering her.

"For some reason I remembered the time my dad pushed me out of the way of an oncoming car."

"Really?"

"I was nine and I chased a ball out into the street," she explained thoughtfully. "The driver never saw me. My dad came out of nowhere and pushed me out of the way. He suffered broken bones and internal bleeding. It took him eight months to walk again."

Art put his hand on her shoulder. "That's what dads do."

She turned and looked at him. "That's what he said."

They started to walk, but Kelsy stopped and asked, "Do you have any kids?"

"Not that I know of," he answered with a laugh.

"I can't believe I didn't know that," she said. "Have you been married?"

Art smiled and jokingly said, "Well, once upon a time when I was skinner, good looking, and taller, I was married to a beautiful little lady."

Kelsy saw something in his eyes that saddened her. Under his joker attitude and his smirk laid something painful. She hesitated, unsure if she should ask him anything concerning his past. "What happened?" her words came out softly.

"I got fat, ugly, and short," he said grinning.

She laughed. "Fine, don't tell me."

Art stared down at the sidewalk and rolled his cigar between two fingers. "I did have a daughter," he said barely loud enough to be heard. "For two minutes and fifteen seconds."

Kelsy could feel a horrible pain swelling in her gut.

"There were complications during the labor," he continued under his breath. "She died on the delivery table and our daughter followed two minutes and fifteen second later."

That was the second Art become an atheist. But then, he met Greg Orfordis and decided to give God another chance to make it up to him.

"I'm sorry, Art," she said as tears fell from her eyes.

Art looked up at her with a shadow of a grin. "It was the best two minutes and fifteen seconds of my life."

Kelsy hugged him, but no words would come out of mouth.

He leaned into her ear and whispered, "I have a new daughter now."

She pulled back and smiled.

"Come on," he said putting his arm around her. "So, what do you expect to find down in North Carolina?" he asked.

She wiped her eyes. "I don't know, but I'm thinking there's something there that may help us get a little closer to our buddy, Hank."

"You don't think he's in the Caymans yet, do you?"

"Nope."

"I got a feeling we're going to end up in the Keys," Art said putting a match to his cigar.

She smiled. "Maybe the Caymans."

"Swing by my place," he said blowing a puff of smoke into the air. "I'll get my passport, just in case."

Kelsy reached into her back pocket. "I'm ready," she said waving her passport.

"You got a change of clothes and deodorant, too?"

They got into the car.

"I heard the Caymans have great Cuban cigars," she said looking over at him.

"You don't say," he said acting disinterested. "Maybe I'll smoke one."

Kelsy looked at him with a warm and sincere glance. "I'll get you one for Father's Day."

14

Los Angels, California

A twenty-two-year-old college student was drinking a beer and shooting pool at the local bar with friends. He was a popular guy on campus: a star player on the lacrosse team, good looking, and a straight A student. His life appeared to be perfect. But there was something from his past that he carried around in the back of his mind. His parents divorced when he was twelve and he was never given an explanation. He was told it wasn't his fault a million times, but the reason for the separation remained a mystery, a dark family secret. His parents hadn't talk about the divorce still to this day. They also never explained why his dad was given custody. He was only allowed to see his mother sparingly when he was younger. By the time he turned eighteen and started college the divorce was old news and never brought up. He and his father got along well throughout the years, but there was always an undercurrent of some sort that acted like a riptide that slowly pulled them apart. His father knew there was a grudge raising within him, but he never addressed it. There were worse things in life people had to live with, and he knew his issue was inconsequential in the big picture. But in his little world, it bothered the hell out of him.

"Hey, Adam," one of his friends yelled across the room.

Adam turned around.

"Isn't that your dad?"

Adam stood and stared at the TV screen over the bar. The CNN newscast was showing minute by minute coverage of the hostage situation occurring on the East Coast. And yes there was his dad, head negotiator of the HRT in perfect HD on the big screen.

15

Baltimore, MD

I started walking back to the command truck after I met with the HT hoping the perplexed sensation I was feeling wasn't showing on the monitors back in the command truck, and certainly not on national TV. I could feel thousands of eyes on me. I knew the media cameras were on me, too. I reached for my cell phone and attempted to look busy as I walked. I realized I had two new text messages waiting. One was from my twenty-two-year old son and the other was from my dad. My son was in college out on the West Coast, so we didn't see much of each other, but we spoke occasionally. My dad lived in Florida. I hadn't seen him in years. My son texting me wasn't really a surprise, but my dad's text was a shock. The thought of him having a cell phone was strange. Oddly enough, both texts read the same, "BE

CAREFUL". I assumed they both saw me on TV. I shot a text back that read, "Always".

I thought about my son and my dad as I walked back. I allowed too much time to pass throughout the years between us, and lost some connection. I know my son held a quiet grudge against me, but there wasn't anything I could do about that. But losing touch with my dad was totally my fault. He was well established in the law enforcement field and did what any father would do, try to help. But when I discovered he was pulling strings to further my career I pulled away and rejected his help. We hadn't talked much since then. I decided I was going to fix that bridge.

I stepped into the command truck and sat the transmitter on the desk. I thought about what the HT said and I tried to process it. I thought to myself, "Call me Mr. Parrot". I stared at the radio as if it were going to magically answer the questions scrolling through my mind. It didn't.

"Sir," one of the operators asked. "Are you all right?"

"Yeah," I answered still looking at the transmitter.

"Everything go OK?"

"Fine."

The other operators gathered around. It was obvious to them that something was bothering me.

"What did he say?" another operator asked.

"He gave me some more instructions concerning the vehicles and he also wants extra clothes, identical to what the men who bring the vehicles are wearing," I said slowly.

The men could sense there was something eating at me.

"Anything else?" one of them asked.

"I asked him what his name was," I said quietly.

The room went silent.

"He said to call him Mr. Parrot."

All of the operators in the room glanced at one another. They were all thinking the same thing. In our world, the vernacular for a hostage taker was "Tango" or "Crow." But there was also another word used in our circle of operations. Parrot was used for a person who had not yet been identified as friendly or a bad guy. The man that held those kids hostage was either trying to tell us something or he was playing major head games.

16

Art slid into the car after filling the gas tank. He placed two large Mountain Dews in the cup holders and a bag of chips on the seat next to Kelsy: the necessities of a road trip. She was busy working the cell phone, trying to gain more information on Robertson. Art merged onto I-95 south, heading for North Carolina. He set the cruise control and allowed his mind to drift. He thought about the death of his wife and baby. Kelsy was the only person he ever told that story to in the last twenty years. He looked over at her and he could defiantly feel a father/daughter connection between them. He grinned to himself. The daughter he never got to experience.

Kelsy was still on the phone. "Hi, I'm Kelsy McKay, I heard you guys had a little trouble with a burglary," she said in her sweetest voice.

Art rolled his eyes.

"Who's this?" the tired voice on the other end asked.

"I represent Mr. Henry M. Robertson," she answered nicely, and then she explained that she was with the insurance company and quickly proceeded to ramble off the policy number and the details of Hank's storage unit information.

The man's tone and attitude immediately brightened. "Great, you're last unit I need to clear."

"You sound glad to hear from me."

"I'll tell you what," the man said, "The sooner this is over with, the better. It's been one big pain in the ass for me. Excuse my language."

"I understand," she said sweeter than before. "I'll be in and out of your hair in no time. I promise."

The man started to laugh. "I'm balder than a cue ball," he said, "but I sure appreciate it."

She laughed and turned on the charm to a nauseating level. "I'm sure it looks good on you."

"I think I'm gonna puke," Art said under his breath.

Kelsy hung up after a few more minutes of sickening kindness and looked at Art. "What?" she asked.

"You sure look innocent," he said shaking his head.

"I am."

"You keep telling yourself that." He turned on the GPS. "What's the plan when we get there?"

"I want to know what's in the unit. If it's the car Hank's going to sell in the Keys, I can add an option to it." She pulled a small tracking device out of her pocket.

"And if there's no car?"

She crunched a chip. "We visit our friends Jack and Paul in the Keys."

* * *

Father's Day

Baltimore, MD

I stepped out of the command truck to get a breath
of fresh air. I just spent an hour getting the run around
from the FBI guys and on top of that, the HT was feeding
the media information via Internet. He told them he
needed the money to pay off his medical bills because his
insurance company refused to do so, and some other
nonsense about losing his house and job because of his
medical condition. "I really could use some good news
right now," I thought. At that moment, I saw William
hurrying across the grounds with a file in his hand. I
looked up at the perfect blue heavens and asked, "Please?"

"Sir," William said handing me the file, "I have
good news."

I guess it was obvious from my expression that I
needed to hear those words.

William laughed. "Did you need some good news?"

"I suck at poker."

"One of the local boys was interviewing one of the
visitors from the aquarium and she remembered the name
of the daycare printed on one of the kid's shirts. So we got
a hold of the center and they confirmed that they have a
teacher and a group of kids scheduled for a field trip at the
aquarium. The teacher's name is Terri Hutch."

I opened the file and removed a number of photos of
the kids and the daycare provider. A majority of the
pictures showed the kids doing daily activities with the
teacher. "Good looking woman."

"Smoking hot," William added, "and according to
her coworkers, one of the nicest people you could meet.

Loves her job, loves kids, and would do anything to help someone."

I glanced at the aquarium and thought about her in there with the HT. I felt a slight quiver of urgency in my gut.

"Check out the other info in there," William said pointing at the file. "They also faxed a list of names to me."

I pushed the feeling aside. "That's good."

"There's more," he said grinning and pointed to a paragraph on a printout. "The teacher is in the middle of a messy divorce and her coworkers said her future ex-husband started some trouble at the daycare before and the cops had to come and remove him from the premises."

I read over the data and my eyes lit up. "Looks like we got ourselves our first person of interest."

"An A1 prime suspect."

I looked up at the sky again. "Thanks."

William gave me an odd glance. "Sir?"

"We need to confirm the teacher's husband info immediately," I said moving toward the truck.

"The FBI has two agents looking for him right now."

I stopped walking and asked, "They already know?"

"They got it the same time I did."

"I started walking again. "Of course they did," I said under my breath.

William walked beside me. "Sir, do you still have a beef with the FBI and Agent Que?"

"No," I answered, "as long as Jay and his boys keep their hands off the steering wheel."

"They said they would let me know when they have something."

"Good," I said and stared at the aquarium. If they can't find him I think I'll have a name for the masked man," I thought.

17

Baltimore MD

The teacher continued to keep the children calm. She already explained to them that the man in the mask was angry at someone else. And when he received what he was asking for he would let all of them go home. The HT heard her conversations and thanked her for controlling the children and then he walked away and stood at the large glass wall facing the city streets. A little girl slowly approached and stood next to him. He looked down at her.

"Why are you wearing that mask?" she asked boldly.

The HT stared down at her and was about to call the teacher over to take her back with the other children, instead he asked, "Why?"

"Why what?" she asked back.

"Why do you want to know?"

She shrugged her shoulders and said, "Why not?"

The HT tilted his head and grinned beneath his mask. "Of course, why not?"

After a moment passed, she asked, "Well?"

"Because I don't want the bad guys to know who I am."

She stared out the large windows at the hundreds of law enforcement people outside. "But you're the bad guy," she said looking up at him.

He smirked under his mask. "Because I wear a mask."

"Yes," she answered as if it should be obvious.

"Do you know who Spiderman, Batman, and Superman are?"

She gave him a look like, "Are you kidding?"

"They wore masks."

It appeared as if she were thinking hard about his last statement. "Superman didn't," she finally said.

"He wore his disguise when he wasn't a super hero."

"A bad one," she said. "Everyone knew Clark Kent was Superman."

He felt himself nearly laugh.

"Are you a super hero?" she asked with a serious stare.

"No," he answered quietly.

"I don't understand."

He looked down at the little girl and said, "A very bad man took something from me and now he has to pay for it." He then stared out the window again at the massive police force. "And they're going to help me." He leaned down and looked the little girl in the eyes. "Now, do you want to know who really is going to help me make things right?"

A.T. Nicholas

"Who?" she asked captivated.

"You and the other kids," he said.

"Really?"

"As long as you and the others stay with me," he explained, "I will get the bad guy."

"Some of the children need to use the bathroom," the teacher said quietly interrupting.

The HT stood and stared from his masked face. "Yes, of course," he said with a low and understanding tone. "Down the hall to the right."

"Who needs to go to the restroom?" the teacher asked.

Half of the children raised their hands.

"Line up," she said.

The HT watched the children line up. One little boy was doing what was known as the pee-pee dance. He obviously had to go badly. The HT had a memory flash through his mind. He remembered a three year old boy taking him by the hand and leading him to the bathroom, and then when they got into the bathroom the little boy made him turn around so he wasn't watching. The little boy checked over his shoulder and proceeded to pee all over the toilet seat. He finished and walked by proclaiming himself a "big" boy now. The memory was gone, but it left a painful ache in his heart.

The teacher started to lead them down the hall.

The remaining children were occupied with a variety of electrical games the HT passed out to keep them entertained.

The HT watched the latest developments on the Internet. One story after another was spreading across the world and it was all about the hostage situation. Parents of the held children were pleading for the release of their kids, others were blaming Muslims, other stories had witnesses attempting to describe the HT, and then there was a group asking for donations to pay off the million-dollar ransom. The images and the voices on the screen started to blur and fade away.

He turned his attention to the children and watched them play and laugh with each other. Something happened that hadn't happened for a long time. He found himself enjoying the moment. The laughter made him happy and there was a rare smile beneath the ski mask, well not a full smile, not even a half smile, more like one-sided grin. But it wasn't long when something inside of him swallowed the moment and sent it into a dark place. He slipped into a numb daze. It was moments later his blank trance was broken by the scream of a woman. He leapt up from his chair and ran toward the source of the scream. Down the hall he found the teacher.

"No, he'll kill the other children!" she yelled.

A man wearing a uniform was attempting to pull her toward an exit. The teacher tried to escape the grip of the aquarium security guard.

"We have to stay and help him get the bad guy," the little girl who spoke to the HT earlier yelled and pulled at security guard.

"Kids," the HT said loud enough to be heard over the commotion. "Settle down."

The children went silent and the teacher stopped struggling. The security guard continued to hold on to the teacher.

When the HT had the children's full attention he said, "Come here, please."

A.T. Nicholas

The little girl started to walk, but the other children looked at the teacher. They were scared and confused.

"Go," she said calmly.

The children walked toward the HT and glanced back nervously at the teacher.

"Go join your classmates," he said with a motion of his thumb.

They merged with the group of children who gathered at the far end of the hallway.

The HT looked down and the little girl was standing next to him with her hands on her hips glaring at the guard. "Hey, he said.

The little girl looked up at him with a serious attitude.

"You got my back?"

"I'll be right here if you need me," she said with eyebrows pulled down.

"I'll be back," he said in his best Arnold Schwarzenegger.

The HT walked toward the teacher and the security guard. The guard pulled the teacher closer to himself. His plan for a heroic rescue was quickly unraveling.

The HT could now see the security guard was unarmed and young, maybe twenty-five. "Let her go and I won't have to kill one of those kids," he said.

The security guard appeared to be in shock.

The HT stepped closer, now a few feet away. "Let her go and you leave."

The guard loosened his grip and the teacher pulled away. She ran to the children.

"Leave," he said.

The guard glanced down at the HT's hands, noticing he didn't have a gun.

The HT knew what the young guard was thinking.

The security guard stood in a state of indecisiveness.

He could see the guard was struggling with his pride and ego. He pulled out his gun and pointed it directly between the young man's eyes. "Does this make it easier to leave?"

The young guard slowly backed away and disappeared out of one of the exits.

The HT walked back to the main room and the little girl walked next to him. "Thanks for your help," he said glancing down at her.

"Was that a real gun?" she asked excitedly.

"He thought so," he said smiling under his mask.

18

Annapolis, MD

A thirty-five-year old man sat in his parents' basement with two of his friends, smoking pot and arguing over who had the better fantasy football team. He was living in his parents' basement because his soon-to-be ex-wife threw him out. She decided a pot-smoking-beer-drinking-comic-book-store owner wasn't the man of her dreams.

An elderly woman answered the knock on the front door. There were two men in dark suits standing on the porch.

"Yes," she said.

They introduced themselves with FBI badges.

The woman was startled by the appearance of FBI agents at her door. "What can I do for you?" she asked somewhat nervously.

"We would like to ask you a few questions."

She invited them in, and asked if they would like something to drink. They declined. "What's this about?"

"Is your son James Peeks?" one of the agents asked.

"Yes," she answered, becoming a little more anxious.

"Is he married to Terri Hutch?"

"Yes." Her eyes widened. "Oh my God, is this about the hostage thing going on at the aquarium?" She had been watching the news all day and knew there was a daycare teacher being held hostage with the children.

"Would you know your son's whereabouts?" the agent asked.

"Yes," she answered. "He's downstairs."

The two agents glanced at one another. That answered one of their questions; Peeks wasn't the HT. Now they needed to interview him and confirm any involvement with the situation.

The woman led the two agents down the stairs to the basement. Of course, the agents immediately smelled the pot.

"Jimmy," the woman yelled halfway down.

"Not now, Mom," Jimmy yelled back.

Jimmy just filled his lungs with a hit when he looked up, and to his surprise there were two serious-looking men staring at him. He tried to pass the bong to his friend.

"I'm good," the friend quickly said, rejecting the bong.

Jimmy began to turn red from holding his breath.

"How long do you think he can hold it in?" one agent asked the other.

"Any second now."

Jimmy released a big cloud of smoke into the air. "Who are you?" he choked out.

One of the agents flashed his badge. "FBI."

"Dude," one of the friends said.

The other agent walked around and studied the room. "Can we ask you some questions?"

Jimmy's mother folded her arms and directed a fractious glare at her son.

"Sure," he said, waving the smoke out of the air.

"Have you spoken to your wife recently?"

"No, why? Is she all right?"

"No, dummy," the mother blurted. "She's being held hostage at the Baltimore Aquarium. It's all over the news."

"I didn't know," he said defensively.

"Damn dude," the friend said.

"I'm assuming you have no involvement with the situation at the aquarium?" the agent asked.

"Are you kidding?" he asked.

"That's messed up dude," the friend said.

The agents were now positive that this man had no involvement with the hostage plot; as a matter of fact they were convinced he probably wasn't capable of any plot.

One of the agents picked up the bong and smelled it. "Colombian Red Bud?" he asked.

Jimmy apprehensively glanced at his friends.

"Dude," one of the friends said.

The agent looked at the computer screen. "You traded Tom Brady for Larry Fitzgerald and Vincent Jackson?"

Jimmy looked over with a curious stare. "I needed receivers," he said attempting to justify the trade.

A.T. Nicholas

"I told you smoking this stuff would make you stupid," the agent said to the other.

His friends laughed. "I told you," the friend said, pointing a judgmental finger. "You don't trade Brady."

"That's messed up dude," the other friend said.

"Ma," the agent said to the mother, "we're going to leave this little situation down here for you to deal with. "Have a nice day."

The other agent glanced over at Jimmy. "Traded Tom Brady," he said, shaking his head with condemnation.

19

Baltimore, MD

The FBI had informed me they had found the teacher's husband and he officially wasn't the HT. Just at that moment, the door of the command truck burst open and William yelled for me to come out. By the time I did, four of my guys had someone on the ground, searching him. When they were finished, they escorted him over to me. I knew immediately he wasn't the HT. He was too short and too chunky.

"Who's this?" I asked

"Security guard," one of my operators answered.

"What's your name?" I asked.

"Darrel Straws."

I noticed he wasn't armed. "Did you have a gun?"

"No."

I was pissed off, but I didn't want to show it. This guy could have set off a domino effect that could have killed a lot of people. I needed him to focus on what happened inside with the HT and not why I wanted to chew him out. "What's your story?" I asked him.

"I was hiding in the basement," he answered, still a little shook up. "I tried to grab the lady and some of the kids, but they wouldn't leave."

"Of course not," I said, putting my arm around him. "You see, if they left with you, he would've killed some of the others."

The guard stared at me, and realized the potential circumstances that his actions may had caused. "I, I, didn't . . . ," he mumbled.

"Did you have any contact with the HT?"

"The what?"

"The guy holding the hostages."

"Yeah," the guard said wide-eyed. "This dude with a mask and a gun showed up. He told me to leave, so I left."

"You saw the gun?"

"Oh yeah."

"Was it a handgun?"

"9mm. I got a really good look at it."

"Sounds like it," I said. "Anything else?"

"Big dude, maybe six-four two-hundred thirty."

"So, all he said to you was, 'leave'?"

"Yeah," the guard said. "And there was no negotiation in his voice."

I walked over to William. "Have the security guy tell you the story again, if anything new pops up, let me know."

William took the guard away.

I walked over and radioed Mr. Parrot, and I hoped he wasn't as upset as I was. Ten seconds passed before he answered, but it felt like an hour.

"I'm here," Mr. Parrot's emotionless voice stated.

"I didn't have anything to do with that." I said.

"I know," he responded. "You're not that stupid."

"Thanks."

"How's the schedule?"

"Everything will be ready when I said it would be," I reassured him. "How's your end?"

"With the exception of the bathroom breaks, good."

20

"Did you eat all the chips?" Art joked.

Kelsy glanced over at him with a chip in her hand and a guilty look. "Not all of them." She ate the chip out of her hand. "OK, now I ate all the chips."

"Chips are fattening by the way."

"You would know."

"And unhealthy," he added smiling.

She shot him a disgruntled teenager glare. "OK, dad," she joked. "I won't eat all the chips anymore."

Art and Kelsy had been on the road for hours. Kelsy gathered more information on the two men in the Keys and Art tried to get some of Robertson's former coworkers from the shock trauma unit to call him back.

"OK, this is what we know," Kelsy started. "Robertson was married and used to be a helicopter pilot for a shock trauma unit. Gets divorced, quits his job, and disappears for nearly a year. Or did he quit his job and then get a divorce?" she asked.

"I'm not sure which happened first," Art said.

"Maybe something happened at his job that caused the divorce."

"I just assumed the divorce came first."

"It really doesn't matter," Kelsy said. "I'm just thinking out loud."

"After the divorce he disappears for a year," Art continued.

"We have no idea what he was doing during that time."

"We know he wasn't living at the house for long, and he left it to his sister to sell."

"He transferred money to a Grand Cayman bank account, and withdrew thirty thousand dollars over a span of two weeks."

"He renewed his passport and bought a one-way ticket to the Caymans with his credit card."

"Then, he canceled the card and all services to the house."

"We know he has a storage unit in Kill Devil Hills, North Carolina."

"And he's supposed to sell a car to someone named Jack and go on a charter boat with someone named Paul in the Keys."

They remained silent for a moment. "Maybe he sells the car to Jack and gets on the boat with Paul and sails off into the sunset to the Caymans," Art finally said.

"Why buy a ticket?"

"Maybe he changed his mind or he might fly out of Miami."

"Do you think we should go straight to the Keys?" Kelsy asked.

"Maybe."

Kelsy's cell phone started to play, Hit Me With Your Best Shot. "Hello," she answered.

"Hey, what's up?" Mary asked.

"What's up, newlywed?"

Art smiled. "What's up, Mary?" he yelled.

"She says hi," Kelsy told him.

"What's going on?" Mary asked.

"Art and I are heading to North Carolina on a missing person case. What's going on with you?"

"Allen and I were sitting here eating dinner, drinking wine, watching the beautiful sunset on the Mediterranean, and Allen had a great idea. He said we should invite you and the others over to join us."

"I love Allen," Kelsy said. "Hey Art, do you want to go to Greece?"

"Yes I do," he answered without hesitation.

"He said he needs to think about it."

"I'll be there," he yelled.

Kelsy was thinking how happy Mary sounded.

"When you're done, call me. We'll work out the details."

"Sounds good."

***

Baltimore, MD

I sat in the command truck staring at the surveillance monitors we placed around the building, but I was thinking about my son. I was second guessing myself again. Maybe I should have told him what had happened between me and his mother. He was a bright and a mentally tough kid, he probably would have understood. We had a good relationship regardless of the resentment he carried around with him against me. But I couldn't help wondering if it could have been better and easier if I told him. I shook my head and rubbed my eyes. I got a bunch of kids being held hostage and I'm thinking about my son's rancor.

"Sir," William asked, standing behind me, "Are you alright?"

"What's up?" I asked.

"I talked to the security guard and he added a few interesting things to his story."

I spun my chair around and waited.

"He said that there was a weird bond between the HT and the kids. Like they were working together"

"That's normal," I said. "There's always a relationship of some sort."

"The guard said something that I found interesting," William continued. "He said one of the kids yelled, we have to stay and help him get the bad guy."

I stared at William and thought about it for a moment. That meant something, but I just wasn't getting it.

"What do you think?"

"I think you're right," I said, buying some time. "It's interesting."

"Maybe the HT has convinced them he's the good guy."

I had a crazy thought. "Maybe he is the good guy." I mumbled to myself.

"Sir?" William asked staring at me.

"I don't know," I said and then stood. "I do know the FBI is on their way and he's going to get what he's asking for." I was thinking about me and my son's relationship again. I was doing the right thing but it appeared to be wrong on the surface.

"Is there anything you need me to do?" William asked.

"Make sure the drivers of the diversion vehicles have escorts to the destinations," I said.

William got on his radio.

I walked out of the truck and stared at the aquarium. There was something different about this situation. I felt like I was on the wrong side. A question in my mind poked me like a finger in the middle of my head. "Is this another terrorist helping another terrorist escape?" I kept looking at the building, waiting for an answer. After a minute, I grinned. "Fine," I said and then pulled on my vest, "I will figure this out and I'll be there at the end."

21

Six men dressed identically sat quietly at one of the café tables in the Baltimore Aquarium. They wore plain dark blue coveralls, black boots, and black gloves and were waiting for the man who chose their clothing of the day. For the last thirty minutes they wanted badly to inspect the envelopes and six blinking devices that sat on the table across the room. The devices looked like cheap digital watches. The temptation to examine them passed through each one's mind, but no one dared to disobey orders. Those orders were simple: Stay put. Stay quiet.

The HT walked into the room wearing the exact same clothes as the six men in the café, with the exception of the black ski mask that covered his head and face. "Don't you just hate it, when you go to a party and some one is wearing the same outfit as you?" the HT asked lightheartedly.

One of the six thought it was funny enough to grin.

"I'm sure you already know why you're here," the HT began. "Just in case you're not clear, I'll explain.

Each one of you will drive one of the vehicles to a destination. Each one of you will be wearing one of those," he said, pointing to the table of devices. "They are numbered one to six. There are also six numbered envelopes on the table. Number one device goes with number one envelope, and so on. Don't mix them up." The HT stepped closer. "Bad things will happen if that were to occur. Each envelope has a destination, and each destination has a device waiting on its match," he said with a nod toward the table. "Once together, nothing bad happens. The box on the floor has masks, wear them before you leave the building."

One of the six men raised his hand.

"Yes."

"Is there a time limit?"

"Yes," answered the HT.

A few moments of uneasy silence passed.

The man raised his hand again.

The HT stepped closer, now only a few feet away. "Yes."

"How much time?"

The HT stared at the man with eyes that only could be described as unmitigated fearlessness. "Enough time for no one to die." He turned and began to leave the room.

"How will we know when it's time to go?" one of the six asked.

"Who has the radio?"

The drivers looked at one another, unsure what to do.

The HT stepped toward them. "I know one of you have a radio." He then pointed his finger at them. "Don't play me for stupid."

One of the men pulled a radio out.

"Channel one," he said and walked out.

* * *

Los Angels, California

Adam Jr.'s cell phone was ringing. He ran out of the bathroom with a towel around his waist, dripping water on the floor. "Hello," he answered.

"Hi, honey," a sweet voice responded.

"Hey, Mom."

"Is this a good time?"

He looked at the puddle of water forming around his feet. "Sure, anytime is a good time for you Mom."

"Did you see your father on TV?"

"Yeah."

"Are you all right?"

"Sure. He knows what he's doing. Are you all right?"

"You know I'm not worried about him," she said and then laughed. "I feel sorry for the man holding those children hostage. He has to deal with your father."

He laughed. His mother always had the utmost respect for his father and his law enforcement career. They both knew he was very good at what he did and he would take care of the situation.

"Well, honey," she said, "I just wanted to make sure you were OK."

"I'm fine," he answered. "Hey, Mom, can I ask you something?"

"Of course."

He hesitated.

"Honey, are you still there?"

"Why did you guys get divorced and dad get custody?" He forced the question out from the darkness of his mind to his lips.

"The line was quiet.

"Mom?"

"I'm sorry, honey," she said catching her breath. "I didn't see that coming."

"I'm sorry, Mom," he said. "Never mind, don't worry about it."

"No, it's all right," she said after collecting her thoughts. "I thought you knew. I thought your father told you."

"He never talked about it. The only thing he ever said was that you guys were better friends than husband and wife, and the only way you could be good parents was to be apart."

"That's true," she said smiling warmly. That was typical of his father. Always protecting. "Well, honey, the truth is that I was an alcoholic and I was also addicted to painkillers."

The line was silent.

"Adam?"

"I'm here," he said catching his breath.

"I had surgery and it didn't go as planned, there were complications. So I turned to alcohol and pills. I couldn't stop. One day when you were young, you nearly drown in the pool because I was . . ." she stopped explaining because her voice began to crack with sadness and guilt.

"Mom, it's all right," he said, attempting to comfort her.

"Sorry, honey," she said.

He could hear the tears in her voice. "It's all right. You were a great mother."

"You nearly died," she whispered.

"But I didn't, and you must have beaten it because I remember you always being there for me."

"Thanks to your father, yes I did. But I missed two years of your life."

"We have the rest of our lives to make it up. Don't forget what dad always says."

At the same time they both said, "Live in the moment."

"I love you, honey," she said.

"I love you, too."

Adam Jr. felt a strange feeling after he talked to his mother. Peace. That little nagging voice was gone. He also felt something else, a new and deeper understanding for his dad's code of honor. He protected his mom's reputation and honor from judgment. He even protected her from her own son. Adam smiled and thought, "Always protecting."

22

I was sitting in the command truck when I noticed the blinking red light on my phone. I was waiting for the FBI guys to show up so I went ahead and checked the text message. It was from my son. It read, "Talked to mom. I owe you an apology next time I see you. She told me everything. Always protecting right? Love you." I stared at the phone screen and got a lump in my throat. I looked around to see if anyone saw my glassy eyes. I sent a text back saying, "See you soon. Love you too." And then, I sent another text to my dad, saying, "I'm sorry for being a jerk and I'll be down soon to see you. Love you." I grinned to myself thinking about my dad reading the message. He might have a heart attack when he read the words, Love you. We never said that mushy stuff to each other.

I walked out of the command truck and noticed the sun had started to sink below the taller buildings. I also noticed a helicopter had landed in the parking lot.

A man in a dark blue suit stepped out.

"FBI," I said to William standing next to me. "Know him?"

"Yup. Special Agent Jay Que."

Two more men stepped out of the helicopter, also dressed in dark blue suits, but not as expensive as Special Agent Que's custom suit.

"Know them?"

"Nope. I bet you one of them is the package."

The package being Abas Majlis, the Scorpion.

The three men started walking toward me. Jay's walk was more like a strut. He was a confident man that bordered on arrogance. But that's what happens when you're good at your job and you know it.

Jay stuck his hand out and I shook it business–like, a very professional greeting from an outsider's perception. We were just two more law officials meeting. But Jay and I have known one another for years and we didn't really care for each other very much. He interfered with one of my hostage situations once in the past. It had a poor outcome. And that didn't sit well with me. Matter of fact, I was still mad as hell at him. He got two innocents killed including the HT. I had the situation under control and he went over my head and ordered the green light. He had two snipers fire through a window, killing two hostages and the HT, and then he refused to take responsibility for the screw up. I would consider two dead hostages a failed mission. But the HT was dead and a dozen other hostages walked away. Jay and the agency thought otherwise.

Jay and I looked at one another and contained our dislike for each other between ourselves, no need to draw any extra attention to the package.

"This is Special Agent Murphy," Jay introduced the man to his right to me.

I shook his hand and introduced myself and then William.

"And this is our newest agent," said Jay of the man standing on his left.

I looked at the so-called new agent. It was Majlis, the man that killed thousands of innocent people, and the man that organized and created the most sophisticated terrorist network in the world. There he was standing right in front of me. "Nice suit," I said.

"Thank you," he coldly responded.

"I was wondering how you were going to deliver him," I said to Jay.

He smiled. "Sometimes the best way to hide something is in plain view."

"Is that my helicopter?" I asked.

"That's it. The new guy and the pilot are going to land on the roof and the HT is supposed to take it from there."

"Let's talk," I said and walked him away from the other guys for some privacy. "What's up?"

"What do you mean?" asked Jay somewhat confused.

I wasn't buying the fake performance. "You're giving up your prized possession without a fight."

"It'll save those kids."

I stared and then I grinned. "You bugged him, didn't you?"

Jay just stared at me, trying to give me his best poker face.

"Does he have any idea?" I asked with a glance at the terrorist.

He shook his head, no.

"Well?" I asked.

He leaned in slightly. "We put a little something extra in his meals every day. The pains shortly followed. We convinced him that his appendix burst and he needed emergency surgery. With the blessing of his attorney we performed the operation." Then a sheepish grin appeared across his lips. "We saved his life."

"Where?"

"Inside one of his ribs."

"Brilliant."

"We'll know where he is all the time," Jay explained, and then his eyes brighten. "There's something else. We can hear him, too."

"I hope it was my tax dollars that paid for that," I said.

"Technology is a wonderful thing."

23

Baltimore, MD

The sky turned a brilliant orange as the sun gradually vanished below the horizon. The silhouette of the helicopter hovered above the aquarium as millions of viewers watched. They sat in their houses, in their work places, in bars, and at cafés. They sat and watched anywhere there was a screen. The United States was dealing with what appeared to be a terrorist hostage situation and the world wanted to witness the conclusion.

"As you can see," the newscaster reported, "it appears the hostage taker's demands have been met."

Every news station had a crew on site and every one of them was milking the ratings. A few of the lucky ones were able to sneak cameras into neighboring buildings, which allowed them to capture the helicopter landing on the roof.

Thousands of people stood behind the police barricade and watched the helicopter slowly touch down on the roof of the aquarium. Once it had landed, some of the news stations switched to camera views located from surrounding buildings. The cameras were able to show the pilot stepping out of the helicopter. There were also hundreds of people recording from hotels and restaurants flooding the Internet with amateur videos.

* * *

The pilot stepped out with his arms up, indicating he was unarmed. The HT waved him over to the rooftop entrance of the building.

"Take the stairs and leave the building," instructed the HT. "Give this to Turner." He handed him an envelope.

The pilot did exactly what he was told and disappeared down the stairwell.

The HT walked into the building and reached for his radio. "Drivers."

"We're here," one of the six responded from the café.

"Start your engines."

* * *

Down in the café, six men jumped to their feet and moved quickly to the table. Every man grabbed his numbered device and envelope. The instructions in the envelopes said they were to wear the watch-like device on their wrists and they were to look at the map they were each given. Each map had a location of the vehicle they were going to drive, and more importantly, the final destination. There was also an ominous note attached to the map. "DON'T TAMPER WITH THE DEVICE. LIVES DEPEND ON YOU NOW," it read.

One of the men grabbed the radio. "We're ready."

A long ten seconds passed before they finally heard the HT's voice over the radio. "Don't forget to buckle up, it's the law."

* * *

In the command truck, I watched the surveillance camera that we hid in the helicopter and I prayed that Mr. Parrot wouldn't find it. I saw him enter the helicopter, close the door, exchange a few words with Majlis, and position himself at the controls. He checked the instruments and studied his surroundings for a moment. He appeared comfortable and familiar with a helicopter.

"He looks like he's flown before," William said over my shoulder.

I watched every little move, every gesture, but I didn't know what I was hoping to see.

Mr. Parrot stood and walked back toward Majlis.

I continued to study his movements and his interaction with the terrorist.

"What the hell!" William blurted out. "Did he just punch Majlis in the face?"

I jumped up and stared at the screen. I wasn't sure if I could believe what I was watching. He was tying Majlis to the chair.

"Sir, what the hell is going on?"

The other operatives moved closer to the screen.

"Where's Jay?" I yelled.

"Outside smoking a cigar."

"Get him."

Jay ran into the truck. "What's going on?"

"The rat with the cheese," I said, "just got his ass knocked out with a Mike Tyson hook and got duct taped to his seat."

Jay stared at the screen. "Son of …." He reached for his phone. "I need a helicopter, now!"

24

I jumped out of the command truck in time to watch Mr. Parrot and Majlis hover over the aquarium for a short moment, and then slowly fade away into the orange and purple southeast skyline.

"We know he's in the helicopter," said William. "Why are we wasting man-power following the other vehicles?"

I was still staring at the sky. "To make sure those vehicles get to where they're supposed to get to."

When I re-entered the truck, Jay was intensely watching his laptop. I stood behind him and watched the little red dot on the screen leave the city limits and head down the coast.

"Looks like the surgery was a success," I said grinning with just a slight hint of sarcasm.

"He's heading south," Jay said into his radio. He answered his phone and listened for a moment. "No!" he barked. "I need him alive."

"Got any guesses, what his guy's up to?" I asked.

"No," he snapped.

My *friend* was somewhat uptight at the moment. I couldn't blame him. His prize possession appeared to be kidnapped by a very unhappy person, and that cute little homing device in Majlis was useless if he were dead.

"Sir," the FBI analyst said, "this is the only audio I have from the incident in the helicopter."

Everyone listened to the steady sound of the rotating blades of the helicopter. I tried to imagine the scene in my head. Then the voice of the HT appeared on the recording.

"What did he say," asked Jay.

The analyst looked at him with a confused stare. "He said, 'nice suit.'"

I laughed.

Everyone looked at me.

"What?" I asked, "That's funny."

"Where's my helicopter?" Jay yelled into his radio.

While Jay was busy yelling at his people, I was chatting with my boys. The plan was to wait until Jay left, and then my helicopter could pick me up. I knew if my helicopter got here first, Jay and his guys would try to confiscate it. I know Jay; we have a history. He had tried to muscle me out of command before and right now he had the look of a man attempting to control a situation quickly going out of control.

The door of the truck opened. "Sir, I was told to tell you all the children and the teacher are coming out of the building."

"Get the parents and their permission for debriefing of the kids, and find out if the teacher has any information that can help us."

Jay's helicopter arrived and he hastily left with his laptop, and shortly after I followed with my own helicopter and surveillance camera.

* * *

We were in the air for two hours, still heading south, hugging the coastline. William and I were watching the surveillance camera in our helicopter. We stayed a good distance behind Jay's helicopter and a half of a mile behind Mr. Parrot's helicopter.

"What is he doing?" William asked. "He got up from the controls."

I watched Mr. Parrot walk back to Majlis. He slid the helicopter's door open. I was getting a bad feeling.

"He's going to throw him out, isn't he?" William asked.

"Jay, are you there?" I asked on my radio.

"What's up?" he responded.

"Are you getting any audio?"

"Why?"

"Why? What, we're not a team anymore?" I asked sarcastically.

"Sure we are," Jay said.

While Jay was explaining the audio difficulties he was having, I was watching what appeared to be Mr. Parrot having a conversation with Majlis. He went back to the controls for a moment and returned with a large bag.

"Hey, Adam," Jay said over the radio. "I should warn you, the HT is slowing down. So don't run into me."

Jay was right. The HT's helicopter was slowing down. I was getting a weird vibe. I had the feeling there was something wrong with HT's helicopter or it was part of his plan. Either way something told me that something was about to happen. As I watched the monitor, that vibe quickly turned into an alarm screaming in my head.

"What's going on?" Jay asked.

At that time Mr. Parrot lit what looked like a flare. Our visual turned bright white.

Jay must have seen the sudden bright light coming from the HT's helicopter. "What the hell was that?" he shouted.

"Jay! Jay pull back!" I yelled. "Jay pull . . ."

And then, it happened: a big, orange ball of fire lit up the night sky.

My pilot banked hard away from the heat and burning debris. I could hear pieces bounce off of our helicopter as we went through a cloud of smoke. I could smell burnt plastic and metal.

"Jay," I said, looking for his helicopter. "Jay."

"What the hell happened?" he yelled over the radio. "Are you all right?"

"Hell no, I'm not all right. A helicopter just exploded in front me. What did you see?"

"The last thing we saw was a bright flash."

"What was he doing before that?"

"Nothing," I said.

William gave me a concerned look. I stared back at him.

"What do you mean nothing?" Jay said, obviously upset that Majlis just blew up right before his eyes.

"Nothing," I said again, staring impassively at William.

"I've got to go," Jay said.

William kept looking at me. "Sir?" he finally uttered.

I rubbed my eyes and shook my head. "What?"

"What are you doing?"

"Find me somewhere to land."

25

Kill Devil Hills, NC

"Looks like a sobriety checkpoint," said Art.

"I had two Mountain Dews and three cups of coffee."

"I'd say you're sober."

Kelsy stopped her car in between the two police cars.

A police officer shined his flashlight at Kelsy and Art, and then into the back seat. "Hi folks," the officer said routinely. "Where you heading?"

"Ocean Island Self Storage," Kelsy answered.

"Do you need directions?"

"No, thank you," she said and smiled. "GPS."

He smiled and backed away. "Have a good evening folks."

"What's going on?" Art asked.

"Have a good night," he said, waving them through.

Kelsy pulled off. "What do you think?"

"They're looking for someone."

"I think you're right."

Ten minutes later Kelsy and Art pulled up to the self storage building. She could see a bald man working the front counter.

"There's your buddy," Art said.

"That was nice of him to stay late for us."

"Us? You mean you."

"It's not my fault I'm sweet and irresistible," she attempted to say with a straight face.

He laughed. "Oh, yes it is."

"Can I help you folks?" the weary man asked.

"Hi, we're here to see Hank Robertson's storage unit." Kelsy said.

The man's face and spirits lifted. "I'm glad to see you guys."

After a few minutes of introductions and Kelsy's over-the-top charming of the man, they made their way to the storage unit. The man reached down to unlock the unit. "What the . . ." he said. "Oh man, not again."

"What?" Art asked.

"The lock," he said, holding the already opened lock. "The unit was fine this morning," he added dumbfounded.

Art examined the lock. "Seems fine."

"I checked all the units this afternoon," he said, still puzzled.

"Really," Kelsy said. "Did you see anyone around today?"

"No," he answered.

"Did you go anywhere this evening?"

"I went home and grabbed a bite to eat like I always do. I was gone for thirty minutes," he said with a shrug of his shoulders. He pulled the lock off and lifted the garage door. He shook his head at the virtually empty space.

"What?" asked Kelsy.

"I always thought there was a car in here."

"Why?"

"Well," he answered looking around the unit, "I saw Mr. Robertson leave a car here a couple of months ago."

"When was the last time you saw him?" asked Art.

"When he left the car."

Kelsy noticed a pile of blankets in the corner of the unit. She walked over and saw a trail of water leaving the pile. She kneeled down and carefully lifted the blankets. "Art, take a look."

"Now that's interesting," Art said pointing his cigar at the site. "Scuba suit." He also noticed the black carry-on bag.

Kelsy borrowed a pen from the man and used it to open the bag.

Art handed her a penlight.

She pushed and poked inside of the bag. "It's empty," she said after she examined all the pockets. She stood and turned to the man. "Do you know anything about this?"

"No idea."

"Do you know what's going on around town?" Art asked.

"What do you mean?"

"We noticed a lot of police activity," Kelsy added.

"It must be the crash," he guessed.

"What crash?" they both asked.

"My buddy told me something exploded right off the shore from his beach house," he explained. "He said he was on his deck and he thought he heard a helicopter flying low to the water and a second later there was an explosion. He said he heard other helicopters, too."

"Where does your buddy live?"

"About a mile south from here."

"When did this happen?"

"A little more than an hour ago."

Kelsy looked at the scuba gear for a moment and then at Art. "The Keys?" she asked grinning.

"I've got my suntan lotion."

26

Kill Devil Hills, NC

We landed at First Flight Airport approximately a mile north of the explosion. A police car was waiting to take William and me to the station. I had briefed the local cops on the situation. They already knew about the hostage situation that had taken place in Baltimore from the overexposure of the media coverage. I explained to the officers that there was going to be a lot of FBI and few other guys in suits running around their town, and it was going to be a pain in the ass. I recruited a few of the local boys for my own personal investigation, which didn't involve the FBI. I told them I was looking for a possible suspect that may have jumped from a moving helicopter, swam to shore and may or may not be attempting to leave town.

As predicted, the town was swarmed with federal agents. The FBI also used the coast guard for their search and recover mission. They had the local police combing the shoreline and questioning the beach house owners. The local and national media got wind of the crash, and it wasn't long before they started infesting the town.

For starters, I had my new team put additional checkpoints at the roads leading out of town. This would be a larger perimeter than had been put in place by the local police immediately after the crash. I also had men checking out any means of transportation leaving town.

A couple of hours passed when I heard through the grapevine that one of Jay's scuba guys had found something, and I heard he was extremely upset about the discovery. When I called Jay, he was defiantly irritated. "What's up?" I asked.

"Nothing good," Jay responded sharply.

"Find the rat and the cheese yet?"

"Got the cheese."

I thought that must have meant the GPS device survived the explosion. "And the rat?"

There was a delay before he finally answered. "Twenty percent."

"Twenty percent?"

"Twenty percent of the rat," he said discouraged. "Hands and arms duct taped to a chair."

"Sorry, buddy. That sucks," I said grinning. Obviously, I didn't care about Jay or his feelings. "Anything on the HT?"

"I'm sure we'll find pieces of him, too."

"What do you think happened?" I asked, fishing.

"I don't know, Adam," he said frustrated. "Some kind of symbolic suicide, maybe the HT had explosives with him for a future terrorist mission that accidentally detonated. Hell, who knows, maybe one of our own shot him down."

The next few hours the local police, coast guard, and the Feds collected evidence that mainly entailed pieces of helicopter. I was on my tenth Red Bull and it was nearing sunrise when I got a little information that I was waiting for. One of the officers working with me discovered a police report on the computer that had been ignored all night. A manager reported a burglary at his self storage company a mile from the crash site. The report stated that one of the units was broken into and a car was stolen.

I got there in two minutes. When I questioned the manager, I discovered the name of the man who rented the unit and the scuba suit. I had a name and a vague description of the car. I calculated that whoever was driving the car had nearly a ten-hour head start. The burglary shortly after the explosion and the scuba gear in the unit where a car was once stored could all be coincidence; but I don't believe in coincidences.

I caught a ride back to my helicopter, which ironically was a thousand yards from the storage building. I left William behind to monitor the local activities and start a network with other law enforcement agencies that were within a ten-hour radius of the crash site while I flew south on a hunch.

27

I was flying somewhere over Florida when William called me with the latest news, and not all of it was good. The good news: a driver was issued a traffic ticket for speeding south of Miami and the description of the car was a close fit to our stolen car from North Carolina. That meant I was heading in the right direction. The bad news: Jay and his boys found out about the storage building and the stolen car. And he was mad as hell at me for not telling him.

Thirty minutes later, I was at a crossroads. I needed to make a decision concerning my flight destination. I told the pilot to continue south. If Mr. Parrot got a speeding ticket south of Miami, then I had to believe he was leaving Miami and heading farther south. At least, that's what my gut was telling me.

William contacted me minutes later and confirmed my gut feeling. William had been quietly networking with the Florida State police and they started a network with all the local town police south of Miami. A sheriff in Key

West found a car matching the description in a used car lot. He reported it to the State boys, and in turn, they gave William the information, and now I had a new destination.

I knew Jay was mad at me already, but now he was really going to be pissed, because I wasn't going to tell him about this either.

28

The early morning sky above the Atlantic horizon began to brighten with a blue and orange light. Kelsy and Art stood on the dock and stared out as far as the eye could see over sparkling ocean.

"Now what?" asked Art.

"I don't know," she answered.

"Do you think he's going straight to the Caymans?"

Kelsy thought of the slip of paper in her pocket. She found it in Robertson's car at Jack's dealership. "I think he's going to Roatan," she finally said.

"Roatan?" He gave her an odd glance. "Like Roatan, Honduras?"

She handed him the paper.

"Not very smart," he said and shook his head, "leaving information like this lying around."

The paper had a name of a person and the word "Roatan" written on it.

"Either he's arrogant or he just doesn't give a shit."

"I was looking forward to the Caymans," Art said.

Kelsy wondered why a man would try so hard to hide his destination and daily activities for a year, and then leave a clue behind. Then again, maybe it was a fake clue. He was hiding something, and maybe now he didn't care anymore. The more she thought about it, the more interested she became. "How do you feel about Roatan?"

"How do we get there?"

A roaring sound filled the sky behind them. A plain, black helicopter was landing in the parking lot.

"Friends of yours?" asked Art.

"I don't think so," she answered, confused by the strange sight.

* * *

I was talking to William about Robertson's banking activities in the Caymans when I started to land in Key West. I noticed a woman and a man standing at one of the docks. After I touched down, I quickly stepped out of the helicopter. They immediately reached for weapons and pointed them at me. I froze and threw my hands up, "What the hell?" I was thinking. I waved my hands and tried to yell over the swirling blades, trying to show them I had no intentions of harm.

My pilot leapt out and aimed his gun at the two. The situation was getting out of control fast.

I told my pilot to put away his weapon. I showed my badge, but my words were drowned out by the helicopter noise.

The woman pulled a badge and yelled back.

I told the pilot to kill the helicopter's engine. Finally, after a long minute of staring at each other, it was quiet enough to hear. "HRT," I yelled.

"FBI," she yelled back.

"Can I come over?"

They lowered their weapons.

"I'm Adam Turner, HRT."

"I'm Kelsy Anderson, FBI."

I looked at the heavyset man.

"I'm just a pawn in life's game of chess," the man said.

"I've seen pawns take down kings," I smirked.

The man laughed. "I'm Art Hanson, PI."

I tried to figure out, what the hell was a FBI agent doing down here already. Or was this some crazy coincidence. But I don't believe in coincidences.

"What's going on?" asked Kelsy.

"I don't know," I said. "You tell me."

"What do you mean?"

"Well, for starters," I said, pulling off my sunglasses, "you guys pulled your weapons out like you're expecting trouble."

"There's a really good explanation for that," Art said.

"We've had issues in the past concerning government authorities," Kelsy added.

"Aren't you a government authority?" I asked her.

"True."

"Would you like to elaborate?" I asked.

Kelsy grinned. "Not on the first date."

"So," Art asked, "what brings you down to the docks today? Fishing?"

I stared at him while I wondered why these two were down here.

"You can trust us," said Kelsy, trying to be cute.

Art laughed, and then whispered. "She's FBI, I wouldn't trust her. But you can definitely trust a PI."

"I'm looking for someone," I said.

"Did this someone," Art asked, "have something to do with the Baltimore Aquarium?"

I tilted my head at him. "Maybe."

"Was that someone supposed to be here?" asked Kelsy.

"I found his car at a used car lot up the street and the owner of the dealership told me he chartered a boat from a guy named Paul."

Kelsy and Art looked at one another.

"Do you have a name of the guy you're looking for?" Kelsy asked.

I paused for a moment and then asked, "What's an FBI agent and a PI doing down here?"

"Looking for someone," Art answered.

"Was that someone supposed to be here?" I asked.

Kelsy grinned. "We found his car up the street at a used car dealership."

"Really," I said and grinned back. I was extremely interested.

"Where did your someone drive his car from?" asked Art.

"North Carolina," I answered. "And your someone?"

"North Carolina," answered Kelsy.

"Why are you looking for this someone?" I asked.

"The someone's ex-wife wanted me to find him," Art said.

"Did he do something?"

"Just disappeared for a year."

"She was worried," Kelsy added.

"Is his name Henry Robertson?" I asked.

"Looks like we're looking for the same someone," said Kelsy.

"Unbelievable," Art blurted out. "Our boy Hank was the guy holding all those kids hostage at the aquarium."

Kelsy looked confused.

"Are you having a hard time believing your guy was responsible for the hostage situation?" I asked her.

"The time frame makes sense," she said, "but the 'why' is bothering me."

"I don't have the why," I said. "So, I can't help you there."

Art pointed his cigar at me. "Would you tell us?" he asked.

I smiled. "I'd tell a PI, not an FBI agent."

"Thanks," Kelsy smirked.

"Not on the first date anyway." I gave the pilot the go-sign. "Well, it was nice meeting you," I said and put on my sunglasses, "but I have to be going."

"Heading for the Caymans?" Art asked me as I turned to leave.

I stopped and turned. I stared at him curiously. Obviously, they already knew about Robertson's bank information.

"I am a private investigator," smiled Art.

"Evidently a good one," I said.

"I have connections," he said glancing at Kelsy.

"I see." I started to leave again.

"You're wasting your time," said Kelsy to my back.

I stopped and took a deep breath and turned back around.

"He's not going to the Caymans," added Art.

It had become apparent to me, they knew more than I did. "So, where is he going?"

"We need a ride," Kelsy said grinning.

I looked at them and contemplated my new position. "Where are we going?"

29

Key West Airport

The pilot talked to the airport attendant and filled the helicopter with fuel. I was busy untangling the red tape with the suit and tie guys at headquarters back in Washington. It appeared the Honduras government wasn't comfortable with an American helicopter landing in their country, not to mention a government law enforcement agency one at that.

Art and Kelsy were on their phones. They had told me about the secret government agencies called the Shadow Government and White Cell and their involvement with them in the past. That would explain their paranoia and quick draw. I personally never encountered any secret agencies, but I definitely ran into enough of the regular agencies with secrets.

Kelsy finished with her conversation and walked over to Art. It appeared something was wrong.

I went over to them. "What's wrong?" I asked.

"I don't know," Kelsy said. "He hasn't told me."

"I was talking to Robertson's ex-wife," Art finally said.

"Has she talked to him?" I asked, feeling some optimism.

"I told her that I may have found her ex-husband," Art explained, "and then, I asked her if she thought he was capable of something like the hostage situation in Baltimore."

Kelsy and I waited for an answer.

"Well," Kelsy asked. "What did she say?"

"In an extremely calm voice she asked me, if any of the children were hurt. I told her I didn't think so. And then she asked if he demanded an exchange for the children, specifically a prisoner."

I tried to keep my facial expressions under control and I wasn't saying anything, but I sure was thinking about a lot of things.

"I told her I didn't have any details," said Art.

"No one was hurt," I added.

Art stared directly into my eyes. "Then she offered an explanation," he said. His eyes were filled with grief and I could tell he was choked up.

Kelsy was listening and I could tell she was thinking hard.

"Did he get his demands?" Art asked.

"I can't talk about that," I said half heartily. I didn't want to get into that part of the story - yet.

"It was a prisoner, wasn't it?" Art asked knowingly.

I stared at Art and waited for him to tell me how much he knew.

"Did this prisoner blow up a government building?" asked Art.

I felt Kelsy's eyes on me. I looked at her and I knew she put the pieces together already.

"Did you know that there were six-year-old kids in that building?" Art asked. "One of those kids that died was named Henry Robertson, Jr."

I stood perfectly still, but my thoughts ran wild. I knew there was something different about this hostage situation. I was trying to wrap my head around the thought that this entire thing was about a father avenging his son's death.

"If you did hand over the prisoner to Robertson," said Art coldly, "I'm not a betting man, but I'd bet my life that that prisoner is dead."

30

Kelsy, Art, and I were flying to Roatan, Honduras for different reasons. They needed closure on a missing person case. I had a fugitive to capture.

During the flight I received numerous emails from William concerning the scene in Baltimore. A great deal of interesting developments occurred after Robertson left the aquarium. Every media outlet had an interview with someone involved with the hostage situation. There were images of celebrations on every news station of parents and their children reuniting. One particular little girl during an interview took credit for helping the hero getting the bad guy. No one knew what she was talking about, but I understood exactly what she meant. There were some incredible discoveries. I read most of them out loud to Kelsy and Art.

The first message read, "All of the children are safely with their parents and guardians. The teacher was unharmed."

Now the next line in the email made me laugh out loud after I read it. "All the explosives were a hoax."

William went into detail about the fake Plastique and the devices that were built with kid's toys and cheap electronic materials.

Art told me he and Kelsy were at Robertson's old house and saw a number of disassembled toys in one of the rooms.

As I read more of how Robertson took over the aquarium and held countless law agencies at bay with a network of bogus explosive devices, the three of us found it amazing and humorous. I also told them about Robertson's demands for the different vehicles and his request for identical clothing, and then how he made them drive to far destinations with explosive devices, which we now know were not real.

The exploding helicopter sure wasn't a fake and that meant he had real explosives at some point, but we wouldn't know the details of what was used until the test results on the downed helicopter were officially filed.

William's email answered one of my questions about the scuba gear. Robertson volunteered through a friend at the aquarium for the shark tank cleaning duties. He was a substitute diver and worked mostly at night, so no one ever questioned his identification. It appeared that he used the scuba gear from the aquarium when he jumped out of the helicopter. He had been a volunteer for nearly a year, which gave him plenty of time to prepare his plan.

Art and Kelsy told me that Robertson was a shock trauma helicopter pilot, which explained his familiarity in the cockpit.

I explained how Robertson got the number one terrorist in the world out of prison and onto a helicopter with him. I told them about Jay and the entire story behind the surgically implanted GPS that would lead the Feds to other terrorist leaders around the world. But the plan didn't entail Robertson blowing him up.

I also told them about what happened in North Carolina with the storage unit and the speeding ticket south of Miami, and the sheriff report on the used car dealer, which led me to the charter business.

Kelsy and Art told me about Robertson's house and the ex-wife, and their experience with the storage unit, Jack's dealership, and Paul's charter company.

Which, of course, brought the three of us together, and now we were flying to Roatan, Honduras.

31

Roatan, Honduras

A man in a plain white tee shirt and cut off shorts sat at the tiki bar staring out at the blue horizon over the peaceful teal sea. The local children were playing in the lazy surf without a care in the world. The sun sparkled off the surface like diamond flakes. The sound of the waves lapping the shore was hypnotic. The noises around him faded and his vision blurred and a memory crawled out from the cemetery of his mind.

He landed his shock trauma helicopter on a small patch of grass in a park two blocks from the explosion. He ran down the street praying; begging God, don't let the building that was bombed be the one his little boy was in. He saw the dust and smoke traveling between the buildings. It looked like a storm cloud had fallen from the sky. He could smell the destruction waiting for him. He turned the corner and stopped in absolute amazement and horror. Half of the building was gone. People were running and yelling, most of them heading his way. His heart pounded so hard that he heard it over the chaos surrounding him. His lungs waited for his next breath of air. He started to run again. He pushed and dodged through the flow of the hundreds of people moving the opposite direction. He grabbed a woman and looked into her eyes. It was his wife. Her eyes were filled with the terror only a parent could understand. He sprinted toward what was left of the building. The local authorities were too preoccupied with the scene to stop him, plus he had his shock trauma unit uniform on. He headed straight for where the daycare room used to be. With bare hands he dug and removed debris like a man possessed. He pushed, pulled, and threw pieces of building aside. His hands were covered with his own blood. He removed a large stone and discovered a small dusty grey hand. He pulled more stones away until he uncovered the tiny body of a girl. He yelled for help as he pulled her from the rubble. He started CPR and the little girl coughed and spit out dust and vomit. A firefighter took her away. A rescue crew of twenty approached the scene and started to help him dig through the ruins. A firefighter yelled, "I got one." He ran over and looked, but it wasn't his boy. That was the moment when he saw it, a small foot with the type of shoe his son wore. A sickness filled every part of his body. He lifted and pushed away a large slab of concrete. He immediately recognized his little boy's face. The site knocked him to his knees. He wiped the blood away from his son's face. The wound on his head was fatal and he knew it. He clenched his jaw and let the tears fall down his face and onto his little boy's body. He glanced at the sky, searching for answers. All the desire to live drained away from his body. He shook his head in disbelief as he stared at his son's lifeless face. His son was gone, and so was his reason to live. The pieces of his broken heart joined the ruins around him and his soul blackened with anger and hate. He wiped his eyes as he pushed the remaining stone away from his tiny body. There was something in his little boy's hand. He reached down and pulled it from the grip of his small fingers. It was a Father's Day card he made for him.

The man's vision slowly returned and the sounds of the present day were back. He continued to stare out at the water, but now his eyes had tears in them. The pain was there and he knew it would always be there. He would have to learn to live with it or allow it to kill him. He closed his eyes and purposely brought back another memory. He started to think about the helicopter and the terrorist.

He was flying the helicopter down the east coast. He left the controls on automatic pilot and walked back to the tied down terrorist. The terrorist attempted to talk to him from under the duct tape over his mouth. He ripped the tape off and the terrorist started to yell in Arabic at him. He didn't understand a word. He removed the mask cap from himself, revealing his face. The terrorist stare at him and asked, "Who are you?" in English. He pulled a knife out and flipped out the six inch blade and without a word he stuck it deep into his calf muscle. The terrorist yelled with excruciating pain.

He stabbed the triceps muscle perfectly, missing the posterior tibial artery. Otherwise, the terrorist could bleed to death, and he didn't want that.

The terrorist composed himself, and through clenched teeth he said, "I'm going to kill you."

He grinned and without hesitation he pushed the knife through the other calf muscle. The blade went clean through the gastrocnemius muscle with ease.

The terrorist screamed again in agony.

He wiped the blood off on the terrorist's nice suit, complements of the FBI.

The terrorist was gasping for air in between the intense waves of pain. Before he could say a word, the blade of the knife pierced through his shoulder.

Another perfectly placed strike, missing the subclavian artery.

More screams. But now the terrorist's eyes weren't angry. The eyes were begging for it to end. "Why," he asked. His question was sodden with suffering.

He waited for that question. He pulled a card out, a Father's Day card. "Do you know what this is?" he asked, as if the wrong answer would get him killed.

"Yes," he answered painfully. "I don't understand."

"My son made it for me." He looked at it while he spoke. "You see, he was in one of the buildings you blow up."

The terrorist saw more than just a man before him now. He was looking at the angel of death. He was a dead man. This man, or angel was going to avenge the death of one little boy. And there wasn't a thing on earth or in heaven going to stop him.

He secured a homemade pipe bomb the size of a shoe box in his lap with a timer. He stared deep into the terrorist's eyes and said, "This bomb contains material from the building you destroyed that murdered my son."

He continued to peer into the terrorist's eyes, reaching down and snatching his soul out of his body. He was going to hand deliver it to hell. He then stood and removed his clothing revealing the scuba suit he wore underneath. "You have sixty seconds to make peace with your god."

The memory slowly sank back into the blackness of his mind. He returned his attention back to the children joyfully playing in the surf. He knew the pain of losing his child would never go away, but now he believed he could live with it.

***

After we landed at the airport, it took us an hour to get clearance from the local government authorities. I was asked to conceal my weapon and change my clothes. I found something that fit from the lost and found department. I officially looked like a tourist with my baggy shorts and colorful Hawaiian shirt. When we left the airport, all we had was a name from the slip of paper Robertson left in the car. We went into town and started asking around. About two hours later, one of the cab drivers told us the man we were searching for lived in a beach house across the island. The driver took us to a small town on the shore. The white sand stretched along side of the road while small storefronts and restaurants occupied every foot of space on the other side. We asked one of the locals about the man, and we were told he was out scuba driving with a class. Art flipped open his cell phone and showed the lady a picture of Robertson that the ex-wife sent him. She warmly smiled and said, "Oh yes,

Mr. Parrot." I grinned. She pointed us to a small bar on the beach. We casually walked up a sandy path and through a row of palm trees. We saw a man in a plain white tee shirt sitting at the bar. I told Kelsy and Art to spread out and cover the exits, but I had a feeling he was done running. I also told them I needed to go in alone from here.

I walked up to the bar and sat close to him, separated by one bar stool. We were both facing the sparkling blue water. I could hear the surf wash onto the beach. The breeze was soft and cool. It felt perfect.

"What would you like?" the bartender asked.

I ordered a beer. Robertson appeared to be deep in thought, lost somewhere in the darkness of his mind, unaware of my presence.

The bartender handed me one of the local beers. The label read, Salva Vida.

I took a big drink from the bottle. I felt like I deserved a beer. I also thought it was the best beer I had ever had. "Wow," I said loudly. "This is great." I took another drink.

Robertson glanced over at me and I was already looking at him. He looked away for a second and then quickly looked back at me again, and locked onto my eyes. He knew exactly who I was.

I had no doubt it was him. I would never forget those grayish-blue eyes staring at me from under that black mask. I smiled. "Hello, Mr. Parrot," I said with a toast of my beer.

Kelsy and Art watched from two different points from outside the bar.

I raised my bottle. "Have you had one of these? This is a great beer."

"You're a long way from Baltimore, aren't you?" he said unaffected by my presence.

I sat my bottle down and leaned in towards him. "I was about to say the same thing to you."

The bartender asked if I wanted another beer because I had already finished the first.

"Yes, please," I said. "I'd like to buy this gentleman another of whatever he's drinking."

"Another pineapple juice, Mr. Parrot?" the bartender asked.

"Thank you," he said. "And thank you," he said to me.

"Straight juice?" I asked.

While he stared into my eyes, it appeared as though a few million memories were turning over in his head. "I drank enough alcohol over the past year for a lifetime," he finally said, but the words didn't come out easy. Then he looked down at his empty glass.

I thought about what his life must have been like since the death of his son. I have a son and sometimes I wanted to kill him myself, but I knew if anything had happened to him, I would be devastated. I also knew if I was in his position I would have done the exact the same thing.

"Do you see that lady over there?" I asked and pointed. "And that man over there?"

"Back up?" he asked.

"They were hired by your ex-wife to find you. She seems to be worried about you." I smiled. "She thought you might do something crazy."

He put both hands around his glass. "Why would she think that?" he asked.

I looked at the small clouds scattered across the bright blue sky. "Some situations lead to craziness."

He pushed the empty glass away and slipped back into the blackness of his thoughts.

"And some situations," I added. "Lead to . . . justice."

Now he was staring at me, and I could see the deep hurt was gone from his eyes, at least for that moment.

I stood and finished my beer. "I'll see you around Robertson," I said. "If I hang around here too long, I may never leave." I threw money on the bar. "Plus I've got a fugitive to find. My FBI sources tell me he's somewhere in the Caymans." I started to walk away.

"Thank you," he quietly said.

I turned around. "Happy Father's Day," I said and left him sitting there, and I hoped that he would find some peace somewhere in those deep thoughts.

Father's Day

A.T. Nicholas
129